JUSTIN CASE

School, Drool, and Other Daily Disasters

By **Rachel Vail**

Illustrated by **Matthew Cordell**

SQUARE
FISH

FEIWEL AND FRIENDS
NEW YORK

I thank the following master teachers, whose wisdom was so helpful in the process of writing this book: Karen Lisa Shain, Amy Liebov, Laura Strausfeld, Kate Chechak, Sonya Glasser, and Karen Kilbane. And send my deepest appreciation to my most enduring teachers: my parents, my brother, my in-laws, my husband, and my sons. —R.V.

SQUARE FISH

An Imprint of Macmillan

ISBN 978-0-312-56357-8

Originally published in the United States by Feiwel and Friends
First Square Fish Edition: May 2011
Square Fish logo designed by Filomena Tuosto
Book designed by Barbara Grzeslo
mackids.com

10   9   8   7   6   5   4

AR: 5.2 / LEXILE: 790L

JUSTIN CASE

School, Drool, and Other Daily Disasters

September 1, Tuesday

Okay, yes. I'm worried.

Already.

I can't help it.

September 2, Wednesday

Seven days to go until the start of third grade. I can't sleep. I'm not getting onto a good schedule. I'm still on a summer schedule. But worse.

Everybody else is asleep. Mom, Dad, Elizabeth — they're all snoring, and I'm still up. Listening. To the silence.

It's very loud, the silence in my room. I'm flopping around my bed, tangling in my blankets. My pajamas are starting to itch. My stuffed snake, Snakey, is giving me an evil look, like he might come to life and bite me.

I know that is not possible and I definitely don't believe in stuff like that anymore.

Just in case, though, I'm now sitting up, with my heart pounding, throwing blankets on top of Snakey. It's not working. I know he's still in there, under my blankets, with his venomous stuffed teeth and glassy eyes.

I'm more awake than ever.

If I don't get enough sleep, I am a disaster.

Sometimes I am a disaster anyway.

And I don't just mean at ball sports.

—

September 3, Thursday

The class lists came — finally!

My new teacher is named Ms. Burns. I don't think that sounds too good. Burns? She is brand-new to the school. I have no idea if she will be nice or mean, old or young, pretty or an evil witch.

Of course I don't believe in evil witches.

At least, during the day I don't.

My little sister, Elizabeth, is starting kindergarten. She got Ms. Amara, my old kindergarten teacher, the best teacher in the entire world.

If I could have Ms. Amara again, everything would be fine.

But I don't.

So it's not.

I have Ms. Burns, who could be anything. She could hate me. She might hate kids with curly hair or blue sneakers. (I should have gotten the white like Mom said to.) Ms. Burns could be a loud teacher. She could be a yeller.

Oh, I hope she is not a yeller.

Third grade will be horrible if I have a yeller for a teacher.

She might make us sit in rows. I might get seated behind my second-best friend, Noah, who is also on the list for Ms. Burns, and who has an extremely large head. If that happens I will never be able to see the board because of that large head of his.

I will fall behind and never catch up. Ms. Burns will think I am stupid. All because of Noah's extremely large head. He will not be my second-best friend anymore, if that happens. I mean it. I hope he got a haircut at least. He has extremely large hair, too.

I have to call Noah and see if he got a haircut.

———

September 4, Friday

Noah's family is away in Ohio so I got their machine.

Mom said to stop worrying about Noah's hair. Obviously Mom never had a second-best friend as large-headed as Noah.

Unfortunately, Mom got the idea to cut *my* hair. She held up a mirror afterward and asked how I liked it. "I hate it," I said, because I looked awful, like an athlete. I don't want to look like an athlete. I want to look more like a journalist or a researcher, more messy. She said, "Oh, Justin."

Elizabeth, who had been in the living room for most of my haircut before she twirled off somewhere, came back in with a big story clogging up her whole wet mouth. She stopped mid-sentence and asked me, "Who are you?" I told her not to be ridiculous, I was Justin, her brother, which she totally knew. She said, "You don't look like Justin."

I told her I had just gotten my hair cut, and that she knew that because she had seen me getting it cut and also I was still sitting on the stool with the black robe on me and my hair in drifts all around the floor.

She squinted and said, "Are you sure you're Justin? You look more like an athlete."

September 5, Saturday

We're visiting Gingy and Poopsie for Labor Day weekend. Gingy and Poopsie are good grandparents except for a few things:

1. They have a cat. Cats walk like prowling predators, like they want to eat my toes for lunch. Even their cat, Mr. Stripes, who is so old his fur looks like it's been through the washing machine.

2. Gingy makes Jell-O. Food shouldn't jiggle, in my opinion.

3. Poopsie keeps yelling at Gingy, "Did you take your pills? Don't forget to take your pills!" and also, "Did you give the kids their Jell-O? Give them some more Jell-O. Justin loves Jell-O!" Poopsie has trouble hearing so he yells all the time in case everybody else has the same problem.

4. We're visiting them not at their house but at their beach condo, where we all have to sleep in the same room because that is the only room.

5. Everybody snores.

6. There could be sharks.

September 6, Sunday

There aren't sharks.

But there is a LOT of Jell-O.

—

September 7, Monday

This morning I couldn't find Wingnut.

I was not being overly dramatic. I was being underly dramatic. How would Gingy feel if she couldn't find the thing she loves most in the world? I wasn't being fresh; I was just asking.

Later, we found him. He had gotten mixed in with the laundry. Phew. Now Wingnut's fur is a little more matted (like Mr. Stripes, but I didn't say so) and he smells soapy, but I don't care because at least he's back. I've had him since I was born and he was a puppy. His ears aren't silky on the insides anymore but I still like to rub them. I felt like not-me while he was gone.

When we got all the sand showered off us and slimy lotion gunked onto us (for our sunburns) and we went into town for dinner, I got the answer to my question.

Gingy would be annoyed if she lost what she most loves.

Poopsie wasn't actually lost or mixed in with the laundry;

he just didn't realize we were being seated and he was reading a book about gardening in the bookstore while we all frantically looked for him so we could eat already.

Gingy called him some names I am not allowed to say.

September 8, Tuesday

Tomorrow is the first day of third grade.

Mom said to focus on the bright side.

Well, Xavier Schwartz is not in my class this year. That's bright.

No. It's not helping. I'm still focusing on the dark side.

Like what if Ms. Burns thinks boys and girls should never be partners? Some people think that, even some kids. If Ms. Burns

 thinks boys and girls have to hate each other, I will never get to be partners with Daisy, who is my best friend, who has shiny soft hair, a quiet voice, and a pet gecko.

So I am focusing on maybe Daisy and I will stop being best friends this year, even though we're in the same class again for the fourth year in a row, all because she is a girl and I am a boy and maybe Ms. Burns will think we should hate that about each other.

A fire engine siren is blaring toward us. I have to decide fast whether to climb down my ladder and wake up my parents so we can evacuate and not get burned up. I'm losing precious seconds deciding.

Okay. The fire engine seems to have gone somewhere else.

Sometimes my heart pounds so hard it feels like it will break my ribs.

—

September 9, Wednesday

Elizabeth twirled in her first-day-of-kindergarten dress as Mom and Dad smiled proudly at her. Mom said, "I can't believe our baby is going to kindergarten." Dad put his arms around Mom and they hugged each other.

I didn't hear anybody say, *I can't believe our older child is going to third grade*, or hug each other about that. Instead Dad said, "Justin, why are you still in pajamas?" and then said the word *hurry*, like, ten times.

I hate the word *hurry*. It makes my stomach scrunch.

I ended up swallowing some toothpaste, which is not, in my opinion, an important part of a nutritious breakfast.

On our way to school, Elizabeth held hands with both my parents and swung between them. I was thinking maybe I'd just take a short break and sit on the sidewalk for about 100 years. But I didn't. I kept going.

Unfortunately.

The way I am staying positive now is pretending I just nightmared the disaster that happened at school after I got to my classroom and that when I wake up, it will be the first day of third grade all over again.

—

September 10, Thursday

No such luck. It really happened.

—

September 11, Friday

There was a mix-up. That's what the principal said the first day. A "mix-up." They put me on the wrong class list. He apologized to us, twice, then bustled down the hall to his air-conditioned office like it was no big deal.

So all that worrying about sitting behind my large-headed, large-haired second-best friend Noah was for nothing. Because I'm not even in his class. Or my best friend Daisy's class, either. Or Ms. Burns's class.

No. I am in the other class.

Ms. Burns, it turns out, does not look like a wicked witch. She looks, in fact, like the complete opposite of a wicked witch.

The opposite of the teacher I actually have.

Ms. Termini.

I am not even kidding. That is her real name.

Say it out loud and you will know why the only way for me to look on the bright side now is to hope maybe we will move soon.

I looked in the newspaper this afternoon for new jobs for

my parents and I think there are some possibilities if they would just keep their minds open about New Jersey.

—

September 12, Saturday

Noah thinks he is in love with Ms. Burns.

There are 179 days left of third grade.

I may not make it.

Noah also said he read an article on the Internet that a kid was smashed into bits by falling off his top bunk bed. He said he sure is happy he doesn't sleep on a top bunk bed.

I don't even know why he is my second-best friend, sometimes.

No movement on New Jersey yet, despite all my arguments.

—

September 13, Sunday

It's Sunday so I am supposed to be relaxing.

I'm not.

First I had to move all my stuffties down to the bottom bunk bed.

Now I'm thinking about what my actual teacher, Ms.

Termini, said when she closed the classroom door that first day, with me in her room instead of where I should have been, next door with Ms. Burns, who has hair down to her belt and also my two best friends in her class.

Ms. Termini said, "Good morning, students, and welcome to the first day of the rest of your life."

Everybody sat very still at that. Even Xavier Schwartz.

Then she said she had only two rules. She held up one long, bony finger and said, "Work quietly, with complete

attention, concentration, and excitement about learning."

Then she lifted a second finger and said, "Treat yourselves, one another, me, and this classroom with respect at all times."

She asked, "Understand?" and looked right at me, like she doubted I did understand. I nodded so fast my head almost rolled off my neck, even though I had already forgotten both rules. They were too complicated. Each rule was like six rules rolled up into one.

I have spent the whole weekend so far trying to remember the rules and memorize them. Because Ms. Termini seems like the kind of teacher who might give us a quiz on her dumb rules. I keep writing them down as best as I can remember but they make less and less sense the harder I try.

—

September 14, Monday

She gave us a quiz.

It wasn't on her dumb rules, at least. It was on math.

Math is my best subject.

I think I managed to get zero answers right anyway, because Mom made me wear shorts today because of the heat, so my thighs got stuck to the chair and when I tried to peel one off, it was only a partially successful peel.

I had to use all my concentration not to scream in agony.

So I had nothing left for math facts.

I may even have misspelled my last name, which is practically impossible to spell even on a good day: Krzeszewski. Today was not a good day. I think I might have added an extra Z or two in there somewhere. That happens sometimes when I get worried.

Most people just call me Justin K., because Krzeszewski looks like somebody fell asleep and their head rolled around on the computer keyboard.

I am thinking of asking Gingy and Poopsie if they would enjoy adopting me. Even Mr. Stripes and Jell-O would be better than this torture.

Also their last name is Jones.

—

September 15, Tuesday

Elizabeth is adjusting beautifully to kindergarten, I heard Mom brag to Gingy on the phone.

She didn't mention if I was adjusting beautifully to third grade.

And she doesn't even know about the gym teacher, Mr. Calabrio, whose muscles stretch his T-shirt out so it looks like a superhero costume. Mr. Calabrio has high expectations for third graders.

14

Gym is not my best subject.

Mr. Calabrio does not look like the type of guy you want to disappoint, though.

—

September 16, Wednesday

Ms. Termini showed us her sheet of Superstar stickers.

They are very rare. She got them in London, England.

Good behavior gets you a Superstar, in her class. The person with the most Superstars at the end of the month wins a prize.

I looked around at the other kids in the class. I knew most of them from the past few years of recess even if they weren't in my class before. I tried to figure out where I ranked of the 22 of us in terms of behavior. I decided maybe somewhere between nine and thirteen.

"Who wants to win the prize?" Ms. Termini asked.

"Me!" Xavier Schwartz shouted, jumping up from his seat.

"Then I suggest," said Ms. Termini, "that you not yell out."

Xavier Schwartz slumped back down into his chair with red circles firing up his cheeks. He's definitely number twenty-two.

"If you are ready to start an amazing third-grade year,"

whispered Ms. Termini, "raise your hand."

I wasn't sure if she meant raise your hand right now, or raise your hand in general instead of yelling out. I have to get good at peeking around.

—

September 17, Thursday

Ms. Burns doesn't give out Superstars for good behavior.

Unlike my teacher, Ms. Termini, Ms. Burns doesn't talk that much about behavior. Probably she doesn't have to, because all the good kids (except me) are in her class. Also, some of them, well, Noah, just sit and stare at her all day because they are (he is) in love with her.

It is disgusting. I couldn't eat my lunch at all because of how he was talking about her all lovesick. And I was very hungry.

My stomach was disruptive and could have gotten me put into time-out. I spent the afternoon hoping Ms. Termini does not have good hearing.

I still have zero Superstars.

Montana C. has three.

I hate Montana C.

—

September 18, Friday

Daisy ate lunch with Montana C. and Montana B. instead of with me.

Still no Superstars for me. Six of us have zero.

I am in the Xavier Schwartz group of Superstar Failures.

—

September 19, Saturday

My stuffed animals are having a war. Nobody is getting along at all. Wingnut has to sleep on my pillow to get away from the fighting, and Snakey, who had been sleeping on the Pillow of Honor (which I made at my cousin Lydia's birthday party last year) because he was the newest stuffty, is in time-out.

His job was to scare off bad guys.

He was scaring everybody else, instead.

And now because it is Mom and Dad's anniversary, they are out to dinner and Elizabeth and I have been left home with Tania, our babysitter, who likes to braid hair and polish fingernails and text her friends on her cell phone.

So now I am stuck in here, in the war zone, otherwise known as my bed, wondering why Mom and Dad are not home yet.

If I had Superstars to give out, my parents would not get any tonight, and too bad if that would hurt their feelings on their anniversary.

—

September 20, Sunday

I'm on a soccer team again.

Dad is the coach. Again.

I don't know where the man gets his hopefulness about my skills and their chances at improvement.

Obviously, not from reality.

—

September 21, Monday

Today at lunch I was sitting with Noah and Daisy and complaining just a little bit about Ms. Termini and her stupid

Superstars. Daisy shrugged in a new kind of way and said, "We're not in kindergarten anymore, Justin. The teachers are just treating us like big kids is all."

Then she spent the rest of lunch talking with Montana C. and Montana B. about how cool it will be to learn cursive, and which letters they already know how to do, when we are not even supposed to know how to do any, yet.

Then they went out to the playground, just the three girls.

I hadn't even unpacked my lunch. I turned to Noah, who was chomping dreamily on his tuna sandwich, and said, "She used to eat slower."

"Ms. Burns?"

"No," I said. "Daisy. Forget it."

I opened my lunch. It was a cheddar cheese sandwich, a banana, pretzel sticks, and a bottle of water. The banana was all bruised and bashed up.

I knew just how it felt.

—

September 22, Tuesday

It's officially autumn.

I'm officially one of the last five kids with no Superstars.

After school I went to hang around at our store. Most

people think if your family owns a candy store you get to eat candy for every meal. It's not true. But you do get good at sorting.

I am an expert malt ball bagger.

Elizabeth was there, too, bragging about how "absodoodley" wonderful Ms. Amara is. I went in the back room to help Dad. Elizabeth is too jumpy to bag malt balls. They end up all over the floor when she tries.

Dad asked me how third grade was going while we filled plastic bags with thirteen malt balls each. Thirteen is a baker's dozen. Apparently it is also a candy store dozen. I told him, "You get Superstars for good behavior."

"Well," he said, "you're an extremely well-behaved kid, so — "

"Yeah," I interrupted. "Except nobody knows exactly what behavior is good enough to get a star." I twisted a baggie tie tight around my first bag.

"A star?" Dad asked.

"Yes," I told him. "A Superstar. That is the thing with Ms. Termini. From London, England."

"She's from England?" Dad asked.

"No, the Superstars are."

"Superstars?" he asked.

"Grrr!" I growled, because that was so totally frustrating how he kept repeating me and getting it wrong when he had to just listen! "Yes, Superstars, which are what you get from Ms. Termini for good behavior! As I told you already! But what I am saying is that it's totally unfair because some people get a star for nice sitting and other people who happened to be sitting just as nicely all day long didn't get one single stupid Stuperstar!"

My arm swung out and knocked over the malt bar jar.

"Justin!" Dad yelled. All the malt balls were rolling in different directions, toward the edges of the table.

"I got it," I said, trying to catch them as they fell. Unfortunately, I bumped into the table as I was catching them. That started an avalanche.

I lunged to scoop up all the malt balls in my arms before they hit the floor. During the lunge, I landed on a malt ball, which toppled me off balance.

I fell hard onto the floor. It really hurt my hip. That's why I dropped the ones I'd caught so far.

Almost all the malt balls were rolling across the floor at that point but two had landed in my lap. I stood up, put the jar

back where it belonged, and gently placed the two safe malt balls inside it.

"Maybe you should go see if Mom needs help up front," Dad suggested, looking sadly around the malt-bally floor.

"Fine," I said, and trudged to the front of the store.

I hate malt balls anyway.

—

September 23, Wednesday

I got a Superstar!

I worked nicely on my math sheet!

Ms. Termini peeled a big, shiny Superstar off the sheet and placed it right next to the *N* at the end of my name, and then she said, "Congratulations, Justin."

"Thanks," I whispered back. I am not a huge fan of talking too much in class.

"You are quite a mathematician, aren't you?" she asked.

I wasn't sure how to answer that kind of question so I shrugged.

Xavier Schwartz, who was moved to the seat in front of me, turned around and looked at me with growly eyes.

I didn't even care.

—

September 24, Thursday

Four kids still have zero Superstars.

I am not one of them.

Phew.

—

September 25, Friday

Ms. Termini told us to "pack up, stack up."

"Pack up, stack up" means put our lunch boxes and notebooks in our backpacks and stand them up beside our desks. Ms. Termini likes things to be neat. The backpacks all have to be on the left sides of the desks. We all have to sit up straight in our seats. When we were ready and quiet, she still waited a few seconds. I could feel myself starting to sweat again.

"I have something important to tell you, students."

We waited. We sweated.

She smiled. "You are doing a wonderful job as third graders. I want to compliment you all. You are already working well together and individually. I can see you are ready for a challenge."

I like to get compliments. But this one sounded a little bit like a criticism. I wasn't sure. Next to me, Gianni Schicci was grinning. But I wasn't. I thought something bad might happen.

I was right.

"We need to make a sign for our classroom door," Ms. Termini said. "It must include all of our names and have a theme. That is your homework."

What was our homework? Uh-oh. My heart started

pounding. What were we supposed to do? Make a sign? Or just think of a theme? What?

Montana C. was raising her hand.

Ms. Termini called on her.

"*What* is our homework, Ms. Termini?" Montana C. asked.

Ms. Termini answered, "I'd like each of you to come in on Monday with a suggestion, written down on lined paper, for a theme for our classroom sign. You may also include a sketch of your idea. Be creative! Use your imagination! You'll present your ideas to the class next week, and then we'll have a vote."

Present our ideas? Out loud? Oh, dread, I thought. *I hate talking in front of everybody!*

"But we'll each vote for our own ideas!" Xavier Schwartz called out.

Ms. Termini frowned at him. He said, "Oops," and then bashfully raised his hand.

Ms. Termini sighed and said, "Xavier Schwartz?"

"Yeah, um. What I already said," he said.

"I expect," Ms. Termini said, "that you are all mature enough to vote for the idea you honestly think is the best one. The student who comes up with the winning idea will receive three Superstars."

"Three!" Xavier Schwartz yelled, and then raised his hand.

"We will have to work on the order of hand-raising and talking, too," she said with a small smile.

Xavier nodded, his hand still up.

"Xavier?" Ms. Termini asked.

"Three Superstars! Wow!"

Ms. Termini smiled. "Have a great weekend," she said. "And good luck!"

I stood up and lifted my backpack, thinking, *I am going to win that contest. I am going to come up with the best idea ever for that poster, and then I am going to win the Superstar contest. I have to.*

I have to.

—

September 26, Saturday

All through soccer I tried to think of a theme.

So far all I have is "getting hit with a soccer ball on your cheek is not good. Especially when your own father, who is the coach, says very unhelpful things like 'shake it off.'"

I don't think Ms. Termini will like that as a theme for our classroom sign.

So I have nothing, and the weekend is halfway done already.

—

September 27, Sunday

Montana C. is in the lead, with four Superstars. If I win the contest, I will be tied with her, and then all I'd need to do is behave really well and be quite a mathematician whenever we get math sheets and I could win!

An idea I had was a math theme. 22 kids in the class, 182 days in the school year, so how many days would our class go to school this year? People could figure it out, like a puzzle. I would do

$$10 \times 182 = 1,820, \text{ then another}$$
$$10 \times 182 = 1,820 \text{ again.}$$
$$\text{Then } 2 \times 182 = 364.$$

And 1,820

$$
\begin{array}{r}
+ \quad 1,820 \\
+ \quad\ \ 364 \\
\hline
4,004
\end{array}
$$

which is cool because it is the same backward and frontward, which is called a palindrome number.

I am totally going to win and maybe get an extra Superstar, it's such a good idea.

—

September 28, Monday

Even before I woke up I realized that I had come up with possibly the stupidest ever idea for a theme for a classroom poster.

Any kids who liked math, like me and Montana C. and Xavier Schwartz, would just figure it out. Four thousand and four days. Wa-hoo. So what?

And kids who didn't like math, like Gianni Schicci and Montana B., would just hate that theme. So it would lose.

And I would lose.

On the way to school, I got poked in the back. By Montana C. "What's your idea?" she asked me immediately. Before I could make something up, she told me hers was seasons. Like for fall, we could each collect a leaf and paint our names on them. I

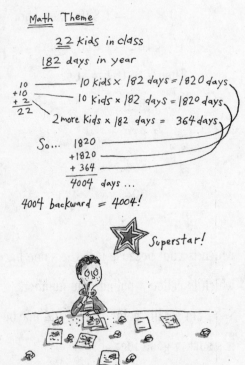

Math Theme

22 kids in class
182 days in year

10 ——— 10 kids × 182 days = 1820 days
+10
+2 ——— 10 kids × 182 days = 1820 days
22   2 more kids × 182 days = 364 days

So... 1820
+1820
+ 364
4004 days ...

4004 backward = 4004!

Superstar!

didn't say anything, so she explained, "For fall."

That's when my dumb sneaker got caught on the sidewalk and I tripped. Montana C. was laughing at me. I considered pretending I was dead.

"I get it," Montana C. said, still laughing. "Fall? You are so funny, Justin!"

Luckily, my great sense of humor (or really, my terrible sense of balance) made her forget to keep asking me about my homework.

———

September 29, Tuesday

Only five kids had time to present their ideas yesterday.

I wasn't one of them.

They were all better than my math idea.

I was slumping, trying to be invisible. The only thing in my head was Superstar, Superstar, and that's when I had another idea. A word scramble of the word *Superstar*:

Rarest Pus.

Ms. Termini called Montana C. up to present her idea. I put a fresh paper silently on top of my math scribbles and wrote on it: Rarest Pus.

I asked myself, how is that a theme?

I waited, but myself did not answer.

Because Rarest Pus is not a theme.

It is just a disgusting-sounding word scramble.

I closed my eyes and prayed for invisibility.

When the bell rang, I realized I'd made it again. But also that tomorrow I was definitely going to have to present an idea, no matter what.

Unless the New Jersey thing could be arranged, fast.

—

September 30, Wednesday

"Justin Krzeszewski?" Ms. Termini called, except instead of saying it "She-shev-ski" like you are supposed to, she said it "Krez-ez-woochi."

Everybody laughed, of course. That always happens, until teachers give up and say "Justin K." like everybody else.

"Did I say it is giggle time?" Ms. Termini growled, and everybody gagged mid-giggle. "Justin, you may present your idea for our class poster," she said.

"N-no," I stammered. "I don't, I wasn't . . ."

"Your hand was raised so nicely, and you were waiting very

patiently, Justin," she said. "In fact, I think you earned a Superstar."

She trudged toward my desk, peeling a Superstar off the waxy backing. I tried to think fast. The truth was, I wasn't waiting patiently, and I wasn't raising my hand nicely. I was twirling my hair. Sometimes I do that when I feel worried. Without realizing it.

Ms. Termini smoothed the Superstar on the other side of my name, before the *J*. Now it looked balanced. I slammed my hand down over my homework paper so she couldn't read my awful ideas for the class poster.

"Okay, Justin," she prompted. "Let's hear your suggestion." She trudged back up to the front of the classroom and picked up her blue pen. She uncapped it and lifted her hand up to number 18, ready to write down my suggestion.

I moved my two papers around, hoping maybe a new, good suggestion might magically appear on one of them. "I had, um, two ideas," I said, stalling.

"Please choose one to share," Ms. Termini said.

"I can't . . . I just, I didn't . . ."

"Justin," she said as her smile melted away. "Please read your homework aloud. We are all waiting. I expect — "

"Rarest pus!" I blurted.

Everybody stared at me. Their eyebrows were all squinched together, their heads all tilted at odd angles.

"Excuse me?" Ms. Termini said.

My face was boiling hot and my heart was pounding so hard it felt like it was going to smash out of my ribs onto my desk.

"Rarest pus," I repeated, quieter, thinking, *Uh-oh. Now what?*

Ms. Termini frowned. "Are you making a joke, Justin? Do you think third-grade homework is a joke?"

"No!" I yelled. "I think third-grade homework is torture! I worked really hard on it all weekend and the only ideas I came up with were a math problem and a thing with, you know, where you scramble the letters and it makes, you know, other words?"

"An anagram?" Montana C. suggested from the front row.

"Yes! I think. An anagram. Rarest Pus I know is not a good theme but it is an anagram of Superstar. And Rarest Pus is all I can think of!"

"All you think about is pus?" Xavier Schwartz asked.

"No!" I shouted. Xavier looked shocked, and maybe scared. I had never yelled in school before. I'd barely talked. I am a nice boy, a good boy, a well-behaved kid. No wonder he was scared. I was scaring myself, too.

"Settle down, please, Justin," Ms. Termini warned. "This is not the kind of behavior — "

"Behavior! Behavior, behavior, behavior!"

Everybody looked scared by then. I realized, too late, that *behavior* is one of those words that starts to sound freaky if you say it more than once. But instead of feeling embarrassed or worried, I just felt angrier than ever that this crazy teacher had turned me into a screaming, babbling idiot, yelling "behavior, behavior" in front of the whole class.

I crumpled up both my papers and threw them on the floor.

"Behavior!" I yelled again. "That is all I can think about! I am trying so hard to have good behavior, I have no idea what else is going on! I can't think of anything except behavior and Superstars! But I don't know what behavior you want, exactly, Ms. Termini. I'm sorry, I can't do it! So, fine. I lose. I am a big loser. I don't care."

I had stood up, apparently, and pushed my chair back. I sat down on it again and folded my hands in front of me on my desk. "That is my suggestion. Rarest Pus. Now please call on the next student."

Nobody moved for a few seconds.

And then everybody did at once.

—

October 1, Thursday

Strangely enough, I did not get punished for getting sent to the principal's office.

In fact, Mom keeps saying, "Rarest Pus," and cracking herself up all over again.

—

October 2, Friday

Xavier Schwartz won for the class theme. His idea was Third-Grade Superstars.

RAREST PUS!

He grabbed me at recess and said he had voted for my idea. He thought Rarest Pus was an awesome theme. Then Gianni Schicci came over, yelled, "Justin K.! You rock!" and gave me a knuckle bump.

Suddenly I am all popular with the kids who get sent to

the principal's office.

It's weird.

Not good or bad, I guess.

Just weird.

Also, I'm sure, temporary.

—

October 3, Saturday

I realized two things during soccer today:

1. I might not be the worst on my team this year, because we have Bartholomew Wiggins to fill that slot. I never had a reason to like Bartholomew Wiggins before.

2. I haven't figured out a costume for Halloween yet. I usually have that all figured out by August. Now I'm way behind.

Even though I spent the entire game working on an idea, I didn't come up with anything good.

My creativity is not what it used to be.

—

October 4, Sunday

Gangs have begun to form.

About half the stuffties on my bed are uniting behind

Snakey. The rest are following Bananas. It is impossible to get any sleep. Wingnut and I ended up on the floor last night.

Xavier Schwartz's mom called my mom today to arrange a playdate for us. I told Mom to say that I am busy this year. Instead she said she would check her book and call back.

There is no way a playdate with Xavier Schwartz ends happy; this much I am sure of. I need to find somebody else to answer our phone from now on.

October 5, Monday

The whole third grade is going to be working on a mapmaking project, with groups combined from the two classes.

The good news is Ms. Burns is in charge of my group.

The bad news is Daisy and Montana C. are in a group with Ms. Termini.

The worst news is my group is me, Montana B., Noah, and Xavier Schwartz. We already got in trouble and our markers were taken away. Ms. Burns didn't think Xavier Schwartz's idea to stick them up his nose was a good one.

It is only the first day of mapmaking and we are already behind.

And my first impression on Ms. Burns is that I am in the markers-up-noses group.

—

October 6, Tuesday

My group is making a map of Europe.

There are way too many countries in Europe.

Group projects stink. Especially when you are in the markers-up-noses group.

Daisy's family and my family always go trick-or-treating together. So even though she hasn't sat with me at lunch in approximately forever, at least there is that to look forward to. If I come up with a really good costume it will give me something to talk with her about and get her off the subject of cursive with the Montanas.

—

October 7, Wednesday

I figured out why it is called cursive: because of the bad words you think when you can't draw the dumb letters right. How many bumps can one *M* possibly have?

Plus, I forgot my lunch today.

Mom brought it up to my class.

As if that wasn't bad enough, she kissed me.

And then she whispered, "I love you" to me.

If my costume for Halloween were "some other kid in my class," I would wear it all the time for the rest of my life so nobody would know I am me, the boy whose mother has to bring him his lunch and then kiss him in front of everybody.

—

October 8, Thursday

Montana C. is having a Halloween party on Halloween.

It's a costume party.

Everybody in the whole third grade is invited. Except all the boys.

Daisy looked at me while Montana was talking about it at lunch. At least she remembers we always trick-or-treat together, always, every single year since we were three. It is a tradition. We will never break the tradition. When we are old, if we live far away from each other, well, too bad on our kids if they have different ideas of what they want to do for Halloween. We always, always trick-or-treat together.

No exceptions.

Daisy looked sad when she looked at me.

I will have to make sure this is the best Halloween ever so she doesn't feel bad about missing that party. I will give her some of my candy, which is not as fresh or high quality as the candy from our store but still it is all mine, and the only time I get packaged candy all year. I'll give her some, though, not even as a trade. Maybe even a big pack of M&M's, if I get one.

Or definitely if I get two.

October 9, Friday

My parents won't get us a dog.

Their only excuse is that I am terrified of dogs.

I tried to explain that I am also terrified of robbers. A dog could scare away the robbers. I would still be terrified of the dog but I could stop worrying about robbers. That would eliminate a whole category of stuff to worry about. Which you would think my parents, of all people, would want to do.

But no.

They were about as convinced by my very logical arguments in favor of a dog, and Elizabeth's jumping, cheering, and pleading, as they were about the whole New Jersey idea.

It seems to me like their minds are just clamped shut with age and rust.

That comment got me a little vacation in time-out land.

—

October 10, Saturday

Bartholomew Wiggins couldn't play soccer today because he sprained his ankle.

I have to find out how to do that.

—

October 11, Sunday

There's a bad guy I might have just dreamed about but I'm not sure. He could be real. I might have read about him in the newspaper, which Dad leaves in the bathroom most mornings and sometimes I end up reading it by accident even though I'm not really supposed to because it's not appropriate for children. Or I might have heard grown-ups talking about him when they thought I wasn't listening.

I get a lot of information these ways.

I am not sure how I learned about this exact criminal.

His name is Bad Boy and he is very powerful.

The truth is, I am not sure even a dog could protect me against him.

I heard him prowling around last night, in the Way-Back of the basement. I am terrified of the Way-Back of the basement. I was there once when I was seven, with Mom, looking at if there was a leak from the chimney. It was dark down there and there were strange hissing and clonking noises and worst of all, something in it called The Boiler. I'm not even kidding. The Boiler. I was thinking The Boiler might be why Bad Boy was back there, Boiling somebody.

I don't want to go to bed tonight in case I hear him down in the Way-Back of the basement again. I may have to find a way to be allowed to stay wherever my parents are, all night tonight.

—

October 12, Monday

They let me fall asleep in their bed, but when I woke up this morning I was in my own. I don't think Bad Boy came by or I definitely would have heard him. Maybe the cops nabbed him, so we can all relax. I'll have to check the newspaper.

Now it's Columbus Day so there's no school and nothing to

do but mope around. Daisy and her family went away. So did Noah and his family. We couldn't because of soccer.

Another reason to hate soccer.

Elizabeth has a playdate over and his name is Buckey. They are hiding under the dining room table and giggling, pretending to be invisible.

When Daisy and I used to play that and hide from her huge gorilla of a big brother, at least we stayed quiet, for goodness' sake.

—

October 13, Tuesday

It turns out that Buckey is Montana C.'s little brother.

Also that Buckey is Elizabeth's boyfriend now.

Montana C. thinks it's the cutest thing ever.

I hate Montana C.

—

October 14, Wednesday

I also hate Xavier Schwartz.

—

October 15, Thursday

I am not allowed to say *hate* anymore. I said, "I hate meatballs" at dinner tonight and Dad got really mad. It is a nasty word, Dad says. It's better manners to say, "No, thank you" if you wouldn't care for any of the meatballs Gingy worked so hard to make.

Fine.

I no thank you Montana C. and I no thank you Xavier Schwartz.

———

October 16, Friday

The reason I no thank you Xavier Schwartz is that when I made the perfectly reasonable suggestion that maybe we should write the names of the European countries in pencil first just in case we messed up, he said, "Justin K., you are the most worried kid I ever met."

"No," I said. "I'm just saying, just in case . . ."

"Exactly," Xavier said. "Maybe that's why your name is Justin Case!"

Everybody thought that was so hilarious. I tried to say, *No, my name is Justin K., short for Krzeszewski,* but of course everybody already knew that, and explaining just made them laugh more and keep saying, "Justin Case, that's excellent! Justin Case!"

I used to wish for a nickname. Not anymore.

People said hi to me more today than the rest of my life combined, which would have been nice except the name they said hi to was Justin Case.

So that is why I totally no thank you Xavier Schwartz.

The reason I no thank you Montana C. is:

Daisy is going to her party instead of trick-or-treating with me.

—

October 17, Saturday

On my calendar it says today is Sweetest Day.

My calendar is wrong.

Dad didn't even care that both my ankles were almost definitely sprained. I still had to play soccer. He said he was sure I could handle it because I am a tough kid and he has faith in me.

He called me "Atta boy." I don't know what "Atta boy" actually means other than too bad on you, you have to play anyway.

Bartholomew Wiggins sat on the sidelines looking at the clouds.

Xavier Schwartz was on the other team. He yelled, "Hey, Justin Case!" at me, and now my whole soccer team, even the two kids who go to private school, call me that.

October 18, Sunday

Poopsie is on Elizabeth's and my side about the dog. "Kids should have a dog!" he yelled as he was eating mashed potatoes.

Mom pointed out that he didn't let her have a dog when she was a kid.

He said she wasn't his grandchild.

She tried to argue that Elizabeth and I are not *her* grandchildren, but he said he couldn't hear her.

I think he can't hear only when he feels like not listening.

Mom repeated herself. Poopsie said she should stop mumbling.

She rolled her eyes at him, a thing that I am not allowed to do.

I like it when Mom rolls her eyes like that. She looks like a kid. I started giggling. She winked at me and gave me a compliment for helping clear the table.

And during dessert, Elizabeth got in trouble for interrupting, finally.

So tonight was a very good night.

—

October 19, Monday

I got a Superstar today.

For my excellent cursive writing.

Hahahahahaha, Montana C.

—

October 20, Tuesday

Ms. Burns complimented me on the way I colored in
Norway.

Her voice is very gravelly.

I can't stop thinking about it.

—

October 21, Wednesday

I asked Daisy today at recess what she is dressing up as for
Halloween. She said she thinks a dog.

I nodded because I was also thinking of going as a dog, so
my first thought was, *Oh, that will be so great, we will be two
dogs, trick-or-treating together*, but then in, like, the
second half of that half second, I remembered that we are not
trick-or-treating together because Daisy is going to horrible
Montana C.'s horrible girls-only party. So we will not be two
dogs trick-or-treating together, we will just be two dogs who
don't even know each other.

Two random dogs.

I couldn't play tag after that. I just sat and broke twigs into
crumbs.

—

~~Dog~~ No!

MONSTER
YES!

October 22, Thursday

I am not going as a dog.

A dog is a baby costume, or a girl's.

I am going to be a monster.

A horrible monster, with maybe blood dripping.

October 23, Friday

We had a spelling test today. I got everything right except *exercise*.

In my opinion a word that ends with the sound *size* should have the word *size* in it.

Another reason to hate exercise. (I mean, no thank you exercise.)

As if Mr. Calabrio with his arms the size of the Hulk's is not enough.

Things I Don't Like:

    1. Spelling tests

    2. Exercise

3. Girls

4. Halloween

5. Limits on screen time

6. The Way-Back of our basement

—

October 24, Saturday

Soccer was great today: The other team didn't have enough players so they had to forfeit, which meant we won! Dad handed out gummy lizards. Everybody thinks he is the best coach ever now. Even maybe me. But we had to keep the whole gummy lizard thing secret from Mom.

That's because Mom is on a health food rampage again. Wheat germ is being sprinkled on everything. Wheat germ is sawdust, only chunkier. Elizabeth and I both keep gagging.

Things I Like:

1. Pretending

2. Counting

3. Helping at the candy store

4. Watching rain on windows

More Things I Don't Like:

1. Being bad at soccer
2. Loud or strange noises, especially at night
3. Runny-aroundy kids
4. Food that jiggles or tastes like sawdust
5. Things that are named The Boiler

—

October 25, Sunday

Last night I woke up in the middle of the night.

It felt like Bad Boy had gotten into my room. I stayed very small and tight in a corner, holding Wingnut against my face for a long time.

Snakey was on the floor beside my bed, but I don't think his venomous stuffed teeth would be a good enough defense.

Mom and Dad have no idea how much we really, really need to get a dog. I don't want to insult Wingnut but what I mean is a dog who is way bigger than he is, and can bark, and is maybe a bit ferocious.

Wingnut is so sweet he'd never even growl, not even at Bad Boy.

—

October 26, Monday

Our maps were due today and ours was not done. We still had the Czech Republic and Greece to do, but we couldn't get going. Montana B. kept giggling while Xavier Schwartz said the word *marshmallows* over and over again, and Noah, as usual, sat with his chin in his hands and stared at Ms. Burns instead of concentrating.

At Montana C.'s party they are going to play games before they trick-or-treat, and there might be a piñata.

I might have to invite Noah and his family to trick-or-treat with us, because if it is just me and Elizabeth, who can't stop talking about Halloween and her birthday party invitations that she sent out this afternoon, I might have to sprain my head and not go trick-or-treating at all.

I will just stay home alone with my lack-of-dog.

—

October 27, Tuesday

I can't even believe what just happened.

I was in the grocery store with Mom, helping to get more wheat germ and other foods not compatible with living human beings, when who came around the corner?

In her jogging clothes, including a top that didn't cover her belly button? And a ponytail? And blue sneakers (a lot like my blue sneakers)?

Ms. Burns, that's who!

And her cheeks were all red. And her eyes were very sparkly.

She said, "Hey, Justin!"

I said, "Ungh."

Mom said, "Hi, I'm Justin's mom." Ms. Burns introduced

herself and said that I am a terrific student, very serious but also very sweet. She said that I have good manners. I apparently say thank you after every class, which I didn't even realize. Mom rubbed my head at that, and then told Ms. Burns thank you and that it was nice to meet her.

Ms. Burns said, "See you in school tomorrow, Justin!"

And I said "ungh" again.

—

October 28, Wednesday

Xavier Schwartz wants to meet up with me and Noah and some of the other boys for trick-or-treating.

I said I'd have to ask my mom, because we might have other plans.

He said he is trick-or-treating with Gianni Schicci, because they always trick-or-treat together.

Yeah, I told him. That's nice. A tradition like that.

He said he wants me to see the costume he's making.

Which reminded me I have to get my own costume together, unless I really do boycott Halloween or get strep throat for it.

Daisy called and left a message that would I please call her back.

Maybe I will, if I have a chance. I am very busy with all my plans for Halloween, though, so I might not.

—

October 29, Thursday

Ms. Burns smiles at me a lot now, ever since I saw her in the grocery store.

Noah says she smiles at everybody the same amount.

He is just jealous.

After that argument, he spent the whole rest of the day bragging about his amazing Halloween costume his dad bought him in the city. It's an alien and has real flashing lights and sound effects.

But mine will have blood, so I don't even care.

—

October 30, Friday

Mom says no blood.

She ruins everything.

—

October 31, Saturday

Well, Halloween is supposed to be scary, so I guess it was a big success.

During the day I had soccer. I pretended my uniform was a costume. I ran around a lot on the field so I'd really look like a soccer star, with sweat and red cheeks, not just shin guards. In

54

the third quarter the ball hit me in the head, which made me really mad. For the first time I just wanted to clobber the ball. I stole it from a kid on the other team and kicked it so hard it hit Bartholomew Wiggins in the butt, bounced over to Sam Pasternak, who is the best player on our team, and he scored. Dad said I get the assist (which is a good thing) and he was all proud of me.

He didn't realize it was just a Halloween costume.

For the night, I dressed as a vampire, with fake teeth but no fake blood. It was okay, though. Mom gelled my hair back and I wore a white button-down, black pants, and the black cape cut off from last year's Batman costume that I didn't even like anyway. It was way cooler than Noah's flashing thing that made him look more like a toy than an alien, but whatever.

We were trick-or-treating near Noah's house when Elizabeth said, after we rang the doorbell of a big white house with pillars, "Oh, I know who lives here!"

I was planning to ignore her because she is always pretending to know stuff she doesn't know, but Mom was like, "Oh, you remember?" And Elizabeth said, "Yes! It's my boyfriend, Buckey, who I am going to marry!"

Just as it was computing in my head that if this really was her boyfriend Buckey who she is going to marry's house, it was also Montana C.'s house, which meant that all the third-grade girls at my school were behind that door. . . . The door swung open.

And there they all were.

They all screamed when they saw us.

That was scary enough. But there was more.

They loaded up our bags with supermarket candy, and then

Montana C. started begging her parents to let them all go trick-or-treating with us right then and they could whack the piñata later. Buckey grabbed his mom's leg and said, "Please! please! please!" like, a hundred times. Montana C.'s parents smiled their very huge smiles at each other and then shrugged.

So that's how Noah and I ended up trick-or-treating with all the girls from third grade, and also my little sister, who skipped along holding paws with Buckey C., in their matching dog costumes.

When we finally caught up with Xavier Schwartz and Gianni Schicci and their parents, I almost didn't recognize them. I had no idea what their costumes were.

So they explained: They were dressed as pus. Rarest pus.

The girls all thought that was so hilarious they couldn't stop shrieking with laughter.

Which might just be the scariest sound in the entire world.

I gave Daisy one of my packs of M&M's before we went home. It was no big deal, really. I had another pack anyway. But she seemed to think it was a nice gesture.

She whispered, "Thanks, Justin. You're the best friend ever."

So the night wasn't a total disaster.

—

November 1, Sunday

Elizabeth ate so much packaged delicious low-quality unfresh supermarket candy she threw up all night.

It was disgusting but awesome. I never knew she could make noises like that.

Luckily we set the clocks back so she has an extra hour to sleep it off.

—

November 2, Monday

There's going to be an election for class representative.

Xavier Schwartz nominated me. I tried to say no, thank you but I forgot to raise my hand so I got in trouble with Ms. Termini and there was my name, still up on the board under CANDIDATES.

I hate when my name is up on the board, even if it is not under the words: UNFINISHED WORK.

But nobody could discuss the problem with me at home, because all we talk about is Elizabeth's luau-theme birthday party, and whether she has to wear shorts under her grass skirt or not.

—

November 3, Tuesday

Montana C., who won the Superstars competition again for October, is also running for class representative. So maybe I have nothing to worry about. She is the most popular kid in third grade.

Even I sometimes like her. I don't want to, but it sometimes happens when I am not paying attention.

—

November 4, Wednesday

Today Dad came home early. He wanted to spend some special time with me. I was thinking, *Awesome!* because there was a game I've really been wanting to play with him on the computer.

But he said no about that.

That wasn't the kind of special time he had in mind.

He thinks I am showing a lot of potential in soccer now, so he wanted to do some extra practices with just me.

Poor guy.

He kept saying stuff like, *Good try* and *That's okay, it didn't hurt too much* and *Don't worry, I have a spare ball* but still, I think by the end of our session he had gotten over his crazy fantasy of my soccer greatness.

—

November 5, Thursday

Xavier Schwartz is my campaign manager. He thinks I would be an excellent representative of our class in the student government. He got a button-making machine for his birthday last year, so he wants to make campaign buttons to sell for 25 cents each, to raise funds for the election. I don't know what we would do with the money we raise but he said trust him, elections are expensive. His mother is on the city council so he knows.

He picked me second on his dodgeball team in gym, right after Gianni Schicci, his best friend and the second-best dodgeball player in our grade after Montana C., who had already gotten chosen for the other team. But still, I am not the third-best dodgeball player in third grade. I am, like, the 27th best, on a good day.

Unfortunately, today was not a good day.

I got out by Montana B. right away. Montana B. looks like a first grader, so little and cute with her pigtails and elfish little self. I would have ranked her, like, 37th in dodgeball. Until today. Maybe I still would; it's just that I sank to 38th. I had to sit on the bench with Bartholomew Wiggins like a total dork until Xavier got me back in.

—

November 6, Friday

Xavier Schwartz says I have to show more of a take-charge attitude.

I said okay.

But what I was thinking was, *I may not be cut out for politics.*

The other thing I was thinking was that, in truth, I don't actually *have* a take-charge attitude.

I have more of a sit-tight-and-hope-nothing-terrible-happens attitude.

November 7, Saturday

I scored!

Holy cannoli, I scored the winning goal in soccer today!

Dad picked me up and spun me around and around.

He thinks the extra practice somehow made the difference. I will never tell him that I was actually trying to pass the ball to Sam and just aimed it badly so it arced into the goal accidentally.

It is a secret I will keep as long as I live.

No reason to ruin a father's one moment of soccer pride in his son.

I scored the winning goal.

We went out for ice cream after, even though we'd already had the after-game doughnuts, and Dad got me two scoops with toppings of sprinkles and gummy bears even though that's a waste of money.

And nobody put wheat germ on any of my food all day.

—

November 8, Sunday

Elizabeth's birthday is in two days, when there is no school because of Veterans Day. I suggested a veteran's theme for her party, and Elizabeth thought that was pretty cool, everybody could come as wounded old soldiers and we could do my idea that didn't get used from Halloween about making blood with ketchup and olive oil, but Mom said no.

Again.

I think she has a horror of blood or something.

So it is still a luau theme.

Which is crazy, because we don't even live in Hawaii.

—

November 9, Monday

Montana C. put up posters already.

They are really good.

Xavier Schwartz says our buttons will be way better, after he unjams his button maker.

Montana C. said her brother, Buckey, can't stop talking about my sister, Elizabeth, and how she is his best

friend and future wife. Montana B. said if they really do get married, Montana C. and I will be related.

The rest of recess was weird after that comment. Montana C. looked as nauseated as I felt. She had to go sit down on the swings by herself for a while, right in the middle of tag. And usually she is an excellent tag player.

—

November 10, Tuesday

Mom thinks it would be terrific if I could please be generous and help out at Elizabeth's party.

I tried to explain that I know nothing about helping out at parties, nothing about luaus, and nothing about these kindergartners.

She said she trusts I will figure it out.

I think that woman is way too trusting.

—

November 11, Wednesday

The party went okay, I guess. They made grass skirts from a kit (and most of them ended up with lots more grass glued to themselves than to the skirt bands) and then danced around to ukulele music while I tried to get them organized to play Pin the Coconut on the Palm Tree.

There was a parrot piñata but when people started whacking it with the bat, Elizabeth freaked out and yelled, "No! Don't kill the parrot!" So Dad had to cut it down from the tree and grab all the plastic junk out and just throw it to all the kids, some of whom were chanting, "Kill the parrot!" until Elizabeth told them they were ruining her party and she would not give them loot bags unless they shut up.

I was proud of that behavior. I think Mom actually was, too, even though she yelled Elizabeth's full name at her.

Then there was a little problem at cake time, because everybody wanted to sit next to Elizabeth for it. A girl named Clementine ended up punching Buckey in the head.

Luckily by then Buckey's mom and sister (Montana C.) had come to pick him up. Montana C. and I had a little chat with Clementine. Clementine decided after the chat to apologize to Buckey and sit sulkily at the far end of the table.

I still hate Montana C. (I mean, I still no thank you Montana C.) but at that moment I didn't. We did a knuckle bump on it and took our cake into the kitchen and ate it together while the kindergartners finished up and got their loot bags. When her mom called her name and said it was time to go, Montana C. said, "Awww," and it sounded like she really meant it.

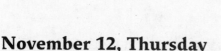

November 12, Thursday

Montana C. sat with me at lunch.

My head felt hot the whole time.

—

November 13, Friday

One thing I do not worry about is Friday the thirteenth. That just seems like a really random thing to get worried about. Daisy worries about it, though. I sat with her at lunch, because I am the only one who knows about that secret worry of hers, so I am the only one who can distract her from it. We made monkey faces at each other and cracked up; we invented a whole monkey family, including cousins and great-grandparents.

It was like old times.

Xavier Schwartz made the buttons. He decided to just give them out for free because apparently there's a rule about selling election buttons in our school. I don't know who comes up with what there should be rules about.

We could have made a ton of money probably. Everybody loves them.

Even Montana C. put one on her backpack, despite the fact that she is running against me. She said, "I don't care. It's so cute!"

I don't really see what is so cute about it. It's just a white background with navy blue writing on it that says:

Justin Case:

Just In Case!

Ms. Termini frowned but when we got back from recess there was her button, hanging on the bulletin board parallel to the names of the kids in UNFINISHED WORK.

—

November 14, Saturday

Dad had a big letdown today at the game.

I was back to being the second-worst kid, thinking music in my mind instead of concentrating on the ball.

He said he was just tired but I think actually he needed some time to himself to get over his mistake in imagining I had developed Soccer Talent. Maybe I shouldn't have misled him about that goal last week.

It's just hard for me to convince myself to try to keep the ball for myself when a kid comes at me, looking like he wants the ball more than anything in the world. Because the truth is, I really feel like he can have it. I'm happy to let him have it. I'll play with it later if I want to. I know I should not be feeling like that and I'd never tell anybody that's how I feel but I really, really do.

Poor Dad.

Luckily, Elizabeth will be old enough to play next year, so he still has a shot at coaching somebody who might like/be good at soccer.

November 15, Sunday

The battle for President of the Bed is raging. I am trying to stay neutral but it is not easy. There are some really evil, underhanded things going on. I don't want to mention names but I had to have a little talk with Snakey and his flunkies about how it is not nice to spread nasty rumors about other stuffties and how they smell.

It is exhausting in my room these days, I tell you.

What I need is a dog.

A dog doesn't care if you win or lose at anything. A dog just loves and protects you, no matter what. I could so use that, and so could Wingnut, who is looking extremely stressed.

I think Mom might be caving, a little.

—

November 16, Monday

Montana C. came in with stickers today.

They say, "I'm sticking with Montana C.!" in rainbow colors.

Xavier Schwartz was so down in the dumps about it, I had to try to cheer him up. He felt like he was letting me down as my campaign manager. When I tried to explain that I really didn't even want to be class representative, he stared at me, and I swear, I think he was about to cry. Or maybe punch me.

I am not sure which would have been worse.

So I had to say, "Psych!" which means just kidding — even though I was definitely not just kidding. But it cheered him up. Just to be sure he was fully okay, I said okay to Knockdown, his and Gianni's new favorite game, which is basically Knock Me Down and Sit on Me.

Maybe it is a more fun game if you are the Knockdowner.

But at least he didn't cry or hit me.

I can't wait for election season to end. I am already way bruised, and according to Xavier this is just the beginning. I am not sure how much more I can take.

—

November 17, Tuesday

Savers of the Universe might sound like a good game.

Trust me, it is not.

—

November 18, Wednesday

Savers of the Universe was a little better today. Xavier thinks I am so fast if I didn't already have an awesome nickname he would call me Flash.

Flash is such a better nickname than Justin Case.

The only reason I was so fast is that Montana C., who is the fastest kid in third grade, was after me, and Noah whispered to me that if she caught me she was going to kiss me.

I ran so fast I almost threw up, and I had to go to the nurse and lie down afterward because my heart was so pounding.

—

November 19, Thursday

Mr. Calabrio apparently saw me running away from Montana C. yesterday. He made me captain today. We are going to have to run a mile for our test before winter break, and he is counting on me to finish in under 12 minutes.

I wish people would just go back to not counting on me. The pressure is too much for a third-grade boy with enough worries already. Especially now that I found out we are going to my cousins' house in New Jersey for Thanksgiving next week.

—

November 20, Friday

Nobody said anything about speeches.

Why do we have to give speeches?

This is called bait and switch, I think. I heard Poopsie talk about that and it is possibly illegal. Ms. Termini could be facing jail time if the cops find out.

I no thank you Ms. Termini but I am still not sure I would want her to go to jail. Though I could not lie if I had to swear to tell the truth, the whole truth, and nothing but the truth in court.

The only good news is that Bananas won as President of the Bed.

Maybe things will calm down on that front, at least.

—

November 21, Saturday

Trophy Day.

I tell you, when that curtain opened up and revealed all

those golden, shiny, glimmering trophies lined up on those tables, I almost cried. I don't even know exactly why. They called us up to  the stage team by team, and when it was our turn, Dad handed us each a trophy.

I know I mostly stunk again this year but I still felt proud, holding up my trophy and smiling while Mom snapped our picture.

I think maybe that's why they have trophies. I'm not sure many of us would play, otherwise.

—

November 22, Sunday

Spent all day trying to ignore the crazy post-Election-of-the-Bed chaos so I could write a speech.

Also trying to stop thinking about having to stand up in front of my class and give the speech.

Also trying not to think about last time I had to talk in front of the class and ended up saying both "Behavior, behavior, behavior" and, even worse, "Rarest pus."

Well, maybe I will be most improved in speaking in front of the class, and will at least get a Superstar. If you are bad at something, like you yell out instead of raising your hand, and then finally you remember to raise your hand one time, you get a Superstar.

If you always raise your hand, you do not get a Superstar for that.

I say it's a crooked system.

But I am not going to give another speech about my opinion of Ms. Termini's teaching methods. I don't need that stress on top of everything else.

You can't lose Superstars, I think, but I guess you never know.

—

November 23, Monday

Montana C. went first.

I have no idea what she said, because there was a buzzing sound in my ears and also I had to go to the bathroom.

But I had to stand up right when everybody finished clapping.

My speech was written on lined notebook paper that I had copied over in my best writing with skipped lines so it would be easy to read.

It still wasn't.

So what I said was not what was in my speech.

I said, "Montana C. would be a great class representative. I don't really know what a class representative does, even. But I'm sure she would be good at it, because she is good at everything. I am good mainly at worrying, which you know because of my nickname, and also by knowing me. But Xavier Schwartz was a very

good campaign manager and made those buttons, which was a lot of work. So, anyway, if you vote for me, then, thank you, but it's okay if you don't thank you the end."

Well, at least I didn't say the word *pus*.

Or pee in my pants.

November 24, Tuesday

I won.

I would ask for a recount, but Xavier Schwartz is so happy he fell out of his chair even more than usual, and he hugged me.

I think it was a hug.

It might have been beating me up, come to think of it, except he was smiling and saying that I rock.

—

November 25, Wednesday

Montana C. was a very good sport.

She congratulated me yesterday, and today she brought in candies in the shape of turkeys and she gave even me some.

It was disgusting candy but still it was a nice gesture.

I should have voted for her, probably. Ms. Termini said in her instructions to vote for the person you think would make the better representative of our class on student council.

I broke that rule.

I voted for myself.

Breaking rules is quite a way to start my career in politics.

—

November 26, Thursday

When we went around the table saying what we felt thankful for, the only thing I could think of was, "I am thankful it is almost time to get out of here, and that we didn't end up moving to New Jersey after all."

I knew that would be asking for time-out for the rest of the year, or possibly no screen time until I turn 21. So I said, "I am thankful to be here with my family in New Jersey," and I kept all my fingers crossed under the table.

My little cousins may not be human. I think they are some other species entirely. They chase each other around constantly, yapping and screeching, and then their mother, Auntie Bryn, screeches at them to stop, but she talks in a whole nother language. I think it may be baby talk, but my cousins (Dylan and Dermot) are not babies, they are four and five.

So maybe it's just alien language.

At the table they were having trouble sitting still so Auntie Bryn gave them spoons to smash into plates, each other, and me.

Then one of them — I think it was Dermot but it is hard to tell because they look exactly alike (both have crew cuts and wild eyes where you can see the white all the way around) — grabbed my Jell-O off my plate. With his bare hands. And slammed some of it into his mouth and let the rest dribble down his chin.

His mom screeched, "Honey bunny, no touchy-touchy! Justin is still nibble-bibbling on his canoodly-bops!" Or something like that.

I had my eyes closed so I wouldn't throw up.

"That's okay," I said. "I'm done."

It was the first true thing I had said the whole Thanksgiving.

November 27, Friday

We slept over.

At my crazy cousins'.

I am officially not speaking to my parents.

I am also officially over moving to New Jersey.

November 28, Saturday

I know that she thought it would be a special treat.

I just don't know why she thought that.

Now Mom is very sorry about the whole thing. I think especially because it gave Dad a terrible migraine so he locked himself in a room alone while we were there until Mom finally packed us up and said we had to get home.

Dad went for a very long run, alone, when we got home.

I'm thinking maybe Mom is softened up for a dog.

—

November 29, Sunday

I have to remember to never ask Mom for something when her bottom teeth are jutting out in front of the top ones.

Especially a dog.

She is usually calm but not all the time, apparently.

—

November 30, Monday

I am not the only one in my family with worries.

Elizabeth was the one nursery-school kid out of her whole class last year who could not sing "Jingle Bells" at the holiday concert. She turned sort of bluish and cried in Mom's lap the entire time. When one of the other moms suggested that maybe Mom ought to get Elizabeth to toughen up a bit, Mom gave her a laser stare and said, "Thank you for your advice."

I thought that other mom might start to cry herself.

It was awesome.

So when we had an assembly today and the principal made

his big announcement about the holiday concert, my only thought was *Poor Elizabeth must be freaking out.*

It even kept me from freaking out myself.

I guess that's just part of being a big brother — sometimes you forget your own panics because you feel that protective of your little sister.

I was a tiny bit proud of that feeling. It made me realize I am really growing up.

—

December 1, Tuesday

Just when you think you know a person, that person gets a personality transplant or something.

It could really shake a person's faith in everybody.

—

December 2, Wednesday

Elizabeth will not shut up about the school holiday concert. How *excited* she is about it.

It is really, really, really annoying.

I was almost even wishing she would get sent down to the Way-Back and then she would fall into The Boiler. And get all Boiled up. But then I felt really guilty. As annoying as she is, I wouldn't actually want that to happen to her. Now if it does, I will feel guilty about it forever. I absolutely do NOT wish Elizabeth would go to the Way-Back of the basement and get Boiled. I want to be very, completely clear about that.

On the other hand, I would so trade her in for a dog.

Honestly, I would trade her in for a Brillo pad.

And I *hate* Brillo pads.

—

December 3, Thursday

Today we had our first meeting of student council.

The first 10 minutes, while we got lectured about what an honor it was for each of us to be on student council because our peers put their trust in us, I was kind of freaking out a little. It felt like way too much responsibility. What if I had to make a really important decision, and I decided the wrong thing? I could mess up the whole year for everybody! They would all hate me — possibly for the rest of my life. We'd be 50 years old and somebody would mention my name and everybody would be all like, *Oh, yeah, that's the guy who messed up elementary school for everybody with his stupid decision on student council in third grade. Why did we ever trust him with that huge responsibility?*

Then I spent the next 10 minutes trying to think of something interesting about myself. Because we were going around the circle saying our name, our class, and something interesting about ourselves.

They didn't say that would be part of the deal when we signed up to run, that there had to be something interesting about ourself.

Not that I had *decided* to run, but I didn't have time to go there.

Two kids before me, all I had interesting about myself was *I don't have a dog* and also a reminder to myself not to say, "Rarest Pus."

What I ended up saying, in a very soft and shaky voice that didn't sound even familiar, was "Justin K., 3B, um, some people call me Justin Case but I don't really . . ."

Nobody heard the rest of what I said, including me.

Instead of listening to what was interesting about all the other student council kids or, after that, paying attention to the bazillion rules and requirements, I spent the rest of the time wishing I hadn't gotten such a great honor and was out at recess with all the less honored kids.

—

December 4, Friday

Noah forgot his lunch.

His mom didn't chase him to the classroom with it.

I said I would share mine, but he said that's okay. He told Ms. Burns and she gave him some salad and baked ziti from the teachers' room.

I am not so sure he actually forgot.

I think there might be a squished-up lunch hiding at the bottom of his backpack.

I bet Daisy would agree with me if she ever sat with me at lunch anymore.

—

December 5, Saturday

What I love about Saturdays in December is the total lack of soccer games.

A kid can just lie on the floor and play video games like a

normal person, for goodness' sake.

—

December 6, Sunday

Elizabeth will not stop practicing her line for the holiday concert.

Her line is, "And we, the kindergartners, welcome you!"

She has tried saying it three billion kajillion ways so far, and is showing no sign of being done saying it. If I get a line, which is the biggest thing I definitely hope I do not get, I might end up saying, "And we, the kindergartners, welcome you!" instead of whatever dopey line is my actual line.

Which would really do a lot for my popularity, let me tell you.

—

December 7, Monday

It is very hard for a person to concentrate in school when he has spent the night before having nightmares about a very dangerous criminal named Bad Boy breaking into his room and doing terribly violent things to his stuffties, who are basically defenseless (even the ones with teeth, because the teeth are soft and can't do much harm despite their ferocious looks), and while he is torturing them, Bad Boy is saying in his horribly sinister voice, "And we, the kindergartners, welcome you!" over and over.

If I failed the spelling test, that is the exact reason.

It is totally Elizabeth's fault.

Studying would not have helped, I swear.

—

December 8, Tuesday

Third graders do a *dance* for the holiday concert.

I am not even kidding.

A dance.

And guess who my partner is?

I absolutely have to get Bartholomew Wiggins to tell me how to sprain my ankle.

Because there is no way I am dancing in front of the whole school, including parents.

Especially with a partner named Montana C.

December 9, Wednesday

Instead of math today, we had dance practice.

And people wonder what is wrong with education in America.

—

December 10, Thursday

I don't even want to think about student council. I don't get it. It's just an extra class so teachers who aren't our real teachers can get a chance to yell at us to pay attention. When we should be playing Savers of the Universe so we won't have less points than every other boy in the whole grade because of missing one out of every five recesses.

Although, during student council, I got a great idea. The idea is to invent a magic pencil that would read the short story tonight for me and then write a one-page reflection about what the story meant to me, in my own words and best handwriting.

That would save me so much time.

Now all I have to do is find Dad's toolbox and make the magic pencil and I will be practically done with my responsibilities so I can finally relax.

—

December 11, Friday

Some people are so sensitive about their dumb toolboxes.

Whatever happened to the whole idea of In Our Family We Share?

—

December 12, Saturday

Bananas is a very good President of the Bed. She really is trying to help everybody get along.

I think she is exhausted.

I am going to let her sleep on the Pillow of Honor tonight for all her hard work.

Wingnut, who usually gets to sleep on the Pillow of Honor, is pouting a little bit about Bananas getting to sleep there tonight, no matter how much I explain that the Pillow of Honor is a special treat and it doesn't mean somebody is NOT good just because somebody else gets to sleep on it occasionally.

Sometimes, as much as I am still terrified of live dogs, I really do think it would be easier to cope with one actual live (drooling, licking, bounding around, maybe even growling . . . yikes . . .) dog than these 87 stuffties, whose problems and complaints and personalities are constantly needing my attention.

—

December 13, Sunday

Noah came over for a playdate in the afternoon. He agrees that we should get a dog, and also that Snakey looks very suspicious. He suggested I keep a close eye on Snakey. I know he meant to be reassuring but that wasn't, actually.

Mom said for goodness' sakes, boys, why don't you go outside it is a beautiful day don't you want to play?

So we trudged outside and sat around for a while until we realized what to play. We played Lawyers in the Underworld, which we made up.

It was fun until it started to rain. Then we came inside and had a snack and wished for snow. I mean, it is December. It should snow, not rain.

We also wished I was in Noah's class. When they do an especially good job, Ms. Burns gives them a reproduction. That means a poster of a famous painting. Noah already has four.

Noah's partner for the dance is Daisy.

He is so lucky.

I couldn't wait for him to go home already.

—

December 14, Monday

Well, that magic pencil would really have been a good invention.

I got a "see me" on my reflection paper.

So now I get to think about that all night.

Goody.

If I had a dog, I would whisper in its ear like I whisper in Wingnut's ear. But a real dog would be a lot more protection than Wingnut, who is missing one eye (the left one) and has had stitches twice. Nothing against Wingnut, who is the sweetest dog in the world, but a real dog would be a big help falling asleep. If it were my own real dog, I would not be afraid of it — or maybe even other real dogs anymore — and I would know that dog would attack any bad guys or teachers who threatened me in any way.

That would be really cool.

Mom said, "Never say the word *dog* to me again."

I tried to pin her down on specifics about the rule, like what if a big teeth-bared dog is running toward her, but she growled and showed her own teeth so I decided I would nail those rules down another time.

Hopefully before anything horrible happens that I could have prevented with that one word. Dog.

Dog dog dog.

I am whispering it to Wingnut, who thinks I might be crazy. Dog dog dogdogdogdogdogdog.

—

December 15, Tuesday

Turns out Ms. Termini liked my ideas.

My ideas made her think of the short story in a different way.

She wanted to be sure they were my own ideas, because she is not interested in Mom's ideas or Dad's ideas. She figures they already had their shot at third grade. She wants to hear my ideas.

They were my ideas.

She said I had a very interesting mind.

Then she gave me a Superstar.

Maybe Vincent van Gogh didn't paint my Superstar, but I don't care. I like it anyway. It feels just as valuable — or more, even though Xavier Schwartz got one later in the day for just raising his dumb hand finally. But I feel like I get the symbolic meaning of mine.

Maybe because of my interesting mind or something.

—

December 16, Wednesday

Now, because of my big fat interesting mind, I am in the highest reading group suddenly.

Now, instead of reading a thing and writing our reflection in one page, I have to read longer stuff and do projects.

Like write a haiku on the theme of change or winter, and a senryu about a topic of our choice. I don't even know what the heck a senryu is.

Everybody else in my group got right down to it.

I was the only one sharpening my pencil twice and looking around at the other groups giggling about Xavier Schwartz and Gianni Schicci falling off their chairs and making monkey noises.

I never realized I could actually miss those guys.

—

December 17, Thursday

How much is there even to say about school spirit?

I mean, honestly. What even is that?

Student council is so dumb.

I shouldn't have worried about making a bad decision. All I get to do is chew on my fingernails instead of play.

—

December 18, Friday

We spent the whole darn day rehearsing our dance.

Montana C. and I ended up stomping each other's feet every time. She started out growling at me the first time it happened but then she kept doing it, too, so I growled back at her. We were more giggling than growling by the time we got our names called out by Mr. Calabrio. Then we got serious fast.

Ms. Burns sat us down and gave us a talk and told us we should think like snowflakes.

That makes no sense at all. Think like snowflakes?

Snowflakes have no brains. Hello.

Daisy made a confused face at me and I made one back.

That was nice.

Montana C. has sweaty palms.

Like me.

It was gross but kind of a relief.

Mostly gross, though. Definitely.

—

December 19, Saturday

I'm lucky my mom is Jewish and my dad is Christian so we celebrate everything. Today was the first day of Hanukkah. Gingy and Poopsie came over for it. Hanukkah is not a gift-giving holiday, really, but according to Gingy and Poopsie, it should be. I think they just like giving gifts.

Actually I think Poopsie really likes buying toys, but Gingy makes him give them to us.

We ate potato pancakes after the smoke alarm quieted down, and then everybody gave out presents. I got a stuffed manatee, which is exactly what I wanted, from Mom and Dad. Gingy and Poopsie gave me a book about knights with excellent pop-ups, and a huge LEGO with 437 pieces. Elizabeth got some other stuff; I don't really know what — nothing I wanted, anyway.

The grown-ups all got clothes.

That is the major reason I am not so excited about the whole growing up idea.

—

December 20, Sunday

For Hanukkah today Elizabeth gave me a whoopee cushion that actually works.

It is the most excellent present she ever gave me.

It made me rethink hating her completely, until she started up again with the whole "And we, the kindergartners, welcome you!"

I told her if she said that one more time I would take back the truck I gave her, which was what she had wanted for her birthday but nobody got her.

Dad said that was not showing the Hanukkah spirit.

Which is not even a thing, I don't think.

—

December 21, Monday

Mr. Calabrio postponed our running-a-mile test until after the holidays so we could practice our dance.

I hope the other grades are better than we are, or nobody will get very holiday cheered, believe me.

Montana C. is coming over tomorrow.

It is not a playdate.

It is to practice our dance for the holiday concert.

I don't care what Xavier Schwartz and Gianni Schicci say, it is not a playdate.

December 22, Tuesday

It was kind of fun.

The not-playdate with Montana C.

But nobody needs to know that.

We practiced and then we played air hockey in the family room, and then we were allowed to have some screen time. She showed me a shortcut I didn't know on Atom Blaster and I showed her one she didn't know, so we both got way further than ever before. Then we had Oreo-eating races.

It was awesome, actually.

Daisy would never shove three Oreos in her mouth at once, no way.

December 23, Wednesday

I didn't fall off the stage and I didn't break Montana C.'s foot during the holiday concert. That's the good news.

Right before we went on, Noah said, "If you get nervous,

just imagine all the parents and teachers in their underwear."

I was nervous already. I yelled at him, "How in the world would it help us if all the parents and teachers were in their underwear?"

Everybody stopped and stood still backstage, and I guess we all tried to picture the parents and teachers in their underwear, and it was horrible and funny at the same time. Daisy started laughing her kind of beeping giggle, which cracked me up and everybody else, too, I guess.

We were laughing straight through our dance, but we got through it. And all the grown-ups kept their clothes on, which, hallelujah, if you know what I mean.

The grand finale was the kindergarten presentation. Elizabeth stood next to Buckey in front. Buckey said, "The grand finale is right ahead!"

Elizabeth took a deep breath.

Nothing came out.

Buckey bumped her with his shoulder.

She took another breath.

Nothing.

Buckey whispered, "And we, the kindergartners, welcome you" to her.

Elizabeth nodded.

She smiled.

She said, "I know, Buckey. Just give me a second to collect myself."

Everybody laughed.

Elizabeth wiped the hair off her face and said, "Phew."

Her teacher, my old teacher, the best teacher in the world, Ms. Amara, nodded kindly at Elizabeth from right in front of the stage, and whispered, "You can do it, Elizabeth. I know you can."

Elizabeth nodded back at Ms. Amara and took another breath.

I slapped myself on the forehead.

Everybody waited.

"And we," Elizabeth said loud and clear into the microphone, "the kindergartners . . ."

Everybody waited. Out of the corner of my eye I saw Daisy smiling her most encouraging smile at my sister. That seemed like a really nice idea so I smiled at Elizabeth, too, and just in time, because her eyes locked onto mine.

"Welcome you!" she finished.

Everybody clapped.

Especially me.

December 24, Thursday

Vacation.

Finally.

My other grandparents, the ones who live in Florida, came today. Ninny and Bop. They are a lot of fun, too, and very, very enthusiastic.

We put up a tree right next to the menorah and Bop played the piano and we all sang Christmas and Hanukkah songs, and some Beatles songs, too, just because Bop likes the Beatles.

Daisy and her family came over for dessert.

Daisy and I put on a show, just for ourselves, with all my stuffties.

We even had marshmallows in our hot chocolates, just like every year.

—

December 25, Friday

Other than not getting a dog, it was a great Christmas.

So I didn't mention the dog thing all day, except accidentally twice.

—

December 26, Saturday

Well, I never expected that.

We do get our biggest Hanukkah presents on the last day, it is true.

But I never expected one this big.

Or this drooly.

—

December 27, Sunday

I know I begged.

I asked and I begged and I pleaded for a dog.

It will just take me some time to get used to him.

For goodness' sake, he doesn't even have a name yet.

 And he is so boundy and jumpy and drooly and looking like he wants to gobble me up for dinner-y.

I am no longer so sure it was such a brilliant idea to get a dog.

Maybe Ms. Termini was wrong about my excellent brain and its interesting ideas.

—

December 28, Monday

Things I Like:

1. Snow, when it falls thick and heavy like today

2. Making a snowman with Noah, even though he gets cold too easily

3. Hot chocolate after making a snowman

Things I Don't Like:

1. When we have to come inside before we are done making the snowman

2. When a dog jumps up on me and knocks me down when I come inside

3. Drool

―

December 29, Tuesday

While Elizabeth and Mom went to visit Mom's cousin Joanie, Dad and I worked at the store together.

Dad called me a malt-ball bagging machine and The Champ.

I even got to work the cash register for an hour, and got three compliments: two about my manners and one about how mature I am.

Dad paid me two crisp dollars, which I put into my cash

99

machine on my top shelf.

I earned those two dollars.

I think I will keep them forever.

—

December 30, Wednesday

Mom wants to name the dog Fluffy.

Elizabeth wants to name the dog Buckey.

Dad wants to name the dog Slobber.

I just want the dog to calm the heck down.

—

December 31, Thursday

The plan I knew about was Noah and his family coming over for New Year's Eve and Noah sleeping over.

The part I didn't know about was that Montana C. and her family and Daisy and her family were also coming over, because it turned out we were having a New Year's Eve party.

We put lots of our best candies out in lots of little bowls, and also real food, but luckily no wheat germ so maybe Mom got over that.

When Daisy came over she fell in love with our dog. The dog is calm and sweet with her, is probably why. Her big brother, Wyatt, sat on the couch and texted on his cell phone and frowned at everybody.

We didn't want to get too near Wyatt, so me, Noah, Daisy, and Montana C. went upstairs to play a game on the computer. Elizabeth and Buckey followed us up there and pretended to be invisible under the desk. Daisy asked me, "What do you want to name the dog, Justin?"

I didn't want to say, *I don't care because I am afraid of this big white fluffy crazy dog I begged to get,* because that would sound so babyish. I stared at my fingers on my computer keyboard and I said, "I want to name him Qwertyuiop."

Because qwertyuiop is just the top line of letters on the keyboard.

Noah and Daisy and Montana C. all agreed that was an excellent name, and we stayed up until past midnight making posters and collars and decorations for the dog that all said Qwertyuiop on them.

—

January 1, Friday

Maybe Mom and Dad had too much champagne.

They thought Qwertyuiop was an excellent name.

So now our crazy dog has a matchingly crazy name.

What a way to start a new year.

—

January 2, Saturday

Qwertyuiop does not get the idea of fetch.

He thinks it means "run around like a lunatic and then knock Justin down with your big muddy paws."

Hahahahaha, what fun.

—

January 3, Sunday

It's not that I am scared of Qwerty.

I played fetch with him.

It was way more than 10 seconds; I don't care what Elizabeth says.

I just had to run inside and have a little time to myself.

There is a lot more homework to do in third grade than in kindergarten, and a lot of expectation that somebody in the highest reading group will read a lot over vacation.

People who think the only reason a person would want to stay in his room with the door slammed shut is because they are terrified of a huge, bounding, crazy (possibly psychotic and life-threateningly dangerous) dog don't know much about life in the top reading group.

—

January 4, Monday

This is the first time I have ever been happy to get back to school after vacation.

Until I saw Xavier Schwartz, who ran over to say hi and knocked me to the ground and then laughed like a lunatic.

I think he may be related in some weird twist of evolution to my dog.

—

January 5, Tuesday

We have to write about what we did over vacation.

I have thrown away fourteen mess-ups already.

Can't we just please, for goodness' sake, move on already? It is a NEW YEAR, people. Let's not dwell on the past.

I bet everybody else did great stuff over vacation.

I bagged malt balls and got a hyper sack of slobber.

That's two paragraphs at best.

And they both stink.

January 6, Wednesday

Xavier Schwartz went to Six Flags. He rode the scariest roller coaster on the planet.

Ms. Termini called him "brave."

Nobody has ever called me brave.

Because I'm not, probably. I'm the opposite.

I'm not just scared of the roller coaster Xavier Schwartz talked about. I'm even scared of Xavier Schwartz.

January 7, Thursday

Ms. Termini called me "funny."

I am not sure if she meant funny ha-ha or funny weird.

I have a feeling it is not funny ha-ha because she didn't laugh when I read my paper of What I Did Over Vacation.

What she did was say, "Speak up, please, Justin," and "We can't hear you if you mumble, Justin," and "I am going to ask you one more time to articulate, Justin."

I finally, finally finished reading my awful homework out loud. Then I stood there, waiting for something to happen. Ms. Termini squinched up her mouth and said, "Well, we all know Justin is . . . funny."

If there weren't a fast-growing monster dog prowling my house, I would definitely fake being sick tomorrow and just stay the heck home.

January 8, Friday

You know what else I hate as much as slobber?

Times tables.

I mean I completely no thank you times tables.

And anyway isn't what a person is panicking about more important than if he says the word h-a-t-e? It would be so nice to have parents who care more about their son's feelings than if he keeps messing up 3 × 8.

It also really doesn't help if a person's parents keep saying the word *concentrate*, either.

Or the words *go to your room until you can keep a civil tongue in your mouth*.

When I didn't even stick my tongue out at them one single time.

And so guess who messed up the threes times tables in school today, after all that time alone in my room not practicing last night?

—

January 9, Saturday

I woke up this morning in the middle of a dream that Wingnut had come to life and was breathing his surprisingly stinky breath in my face.

When I opened my eyes it took me a second to figure out that it wasn't Wingnut breathing his surprisingly stinky breath on my face.

It was Qwerty.

I screamed.

What kind of lunatic dog thinks the best thing to do to a kid screaming in terror and yelling "get away, get away" is to jump on top of him and pin him down with your big heavy paws and lick his face like it's a doggy lollipop?

I am sleeping in the top bunk from now on, I don't care about the risk of falling off and smashing into bits anymore.

I have a sneaking suspicion Noah made that up, anyway.

—

January 10, Sunday

Every time I fell asleep, I jolted awake, because it felt like I was falling off the bed. I ended up building a stuffties barrier, just in case the wooden fence thing and wedging myself against the wall wasn't enough protection. Some of the stuffties (I don't want to mention any names) were insulted at being used as a barrier, and had a bajillion snide comments they felt they had to make about the situation all night long.

This morning Dad said I looked like I needed a cup of coffee.

Mom said she signed me up for basketball.

Also, violin lessons.

As if I didn't already have enough to worry about with the mile test tomorrow.

—

January 11, Monday

A mile is very, very far.

Especially when it is, like, a bajillion laps around the gym.

And you only have 23 minutes and you aren't sure if you already did lap 17 or if 17 is next and also you get a cramp and your sneakers are suddenly squishing your feet. Which means a blister. A biggie, right on the big toe.

But there is good news:

I did it.

I ran the mile, or maybe a mile plus one lap.

Now I never have to do it again.

And then, at lunch, there was even more good news:

I'm in a club! I was one of the first ones asked into it!

—

January 12, Tuesday

Terrible news.

The club I am in is not really a club. It is more of a "we

don't care that you won't let us in your club, we have our own club" club.

The other club has a no boys allowed policy.

Which I actually think is illegal. "Yeah, you tell 'em, Justin Case," all the boys behind me said, or stuff like that, and a lot of "Yeah!" words.

Montana C. disagreed. And, she said, her mom is a lawyer and her dad is a police officer. She had her hands in fists on her hips.

I thought of saying, *So what, my parents own a candy store, so now only the boys can have candy.* But maybe her dad could get me arrested and her mom could get me locked up in jail, and anyway anybody who wants can buy candy at our store. I got in trouble one time last year for telling Noah he could never have any more candy in his life if he didn't let me play with his LEGO car. And no boys were saying, "So what?" or even "Yeah!" anymore. They were shrugging and walking away to the far side of the playground.

Anyway it didn't matter because we don't want to be in their dumb club. We would rather do cool boy things instead of dumb girl things.

Mostly the cool boy thing we did after that was hang

around grumbling about how much we don't care about not being in their loser club.

—

January 13, Wednesday

Dad lost his running shoes. Not shoes, actually, just the left one.

And he thought I made a big deal when I lost Wingnut.

He made it seem like maybe Elizabeth and I stole it to use as a clubhouse or something.

We got out of his way and hung around together in my top bunk for a while. I think kindergarten is good for Elizabeth. She's less annoying than she used to be.

—

January 14, Thursday

Snow day! Finally! And the best part is, it happened on a student council day!

Also a times tables test day!

The snow was pretty much melted by lunch, but still, a snow day is a snow day, and Elizabeth and I and then Noah made a snow, well, not man exactly. More like a snow pyramid, with a carrot and some rocks and sticks in it.

But Noah didn't get too cold, and Mom let us have as many marshmallows as we wanted in our hot chocolates and then sled down Noah's hill until all the snow was gone and we were basically sledding on grass.

I love snow days.

Also, marshmallows.

—

January 15, Friday

What I Do Not Love:

1. $3 \times 8 = 24$

2. Being in the lowest math group, when math is my best thing

3. Sitting down when I don't say that $3 \times 8 = 24$ fast enough

4. Looking around and seeing only Xavier Schwartz and Gianni Schicci are also sitting

5. Dogs

6. Drool

7. The Way-Back of the basement

8. Violins

9. Basketball

—

January 16, Saturday

10. (new addition to my list) My basketball coach whose name is:

Mr. Calabrio

—

January 17, Sunday

Tomorrow is Dr. Martin Luther King Jr. Day, the day when we are supposed to be celebrating freedom for everybody — *not* getting pounded. But too bad for me, because Xavier Schwartz wants me to come over tomorrow.

Or at least his mother does.

And my mother is making me go. She said she is out of excuses and to stop running away from the dog because it "riles him up."

As if that devil dog ever got riled down.

Supposedly me and Xavier are going to work on our times tables together. I tried to point out that since we both stink at our times tables it probably will not help us any. Mom said moaning gives her a headache and she needed to go take Qwerty for a run. Usually Dad takes Qwerty for his run, but it turned out Qwerty had enjoyed Dad's left running shoe as a snack, so he can't go for a run until tomorrow, when he buys a new pair. The old one was covered with dog slime and hidden behind the couch. Elizabeth found it. It was totally disgusting.

Now maybe they see what I mean about dogs and their teeth.

—

January 18, Monday

Qwerty ate up the garbage last night. Now he will have to sleep in the downstairs bathroom. So maybe I will actually be able to go to sleep again.

I could have used a solid night's sleep last night, because

today I have the dreaded playdate of doom. I just hope Xavier Schwartz's big brother is not going to be there. His big brother is the inventor of the game called Tackle.

—

January 19, Tuesday

Xavier Schwartz's big brother was there.

The good news is now Xavier Schwartz is not the Schwartz I am most afraid of.

The bad news is the game of Tackle is rougher than it sounds.

When Mom picked me up I got ready faster than ever. As we left I was saying, "Bye! Thanks! That was great! See you in school! Thanks for having me!" All the stuff Mom makes me say. But as soon as that door shut behind us and we were walking alone to our car, I turned to Mom and said, "Never send me there again."

She could tell I meant it because she said "okay" right away, before she even asked what happened.

Or maybe she had bigger fish to fry. Qwerty got into the bathtub last night and managed to turn on the water and flood the whole room. Now they have to get the floor redone in there, Mom said. She spent the day on the Internet looking at tiles, training methods, and dog cages. Now Qwerty has to sleep in a cage in the kitchen.

I feel a little bad for him, though also I must admit a little relieved.

—

January 20, Wednesday

Elizabeth showed me a project she made in honor of Dr. Martin Luther King Jr. Day, to ask my opinion on whether it was good enough to show her teacher, Ms. Amara, because she wants Ms. Amara to be proud of her.

The picture she drew of Dr. Martin Luther King Jr. was pretty good, especially for a kindergartner. I told her that first, before I read what she'd written. There were a couple of problems with that part.

For one thing, Elizabeth wrote his name as "Martin the King." And after that she just wrote "Martin" because, she said, her hand was getting tired from so many letters.

The other problem was that she wrote, "Martin the King was a hero because he fought to change a very, very stupid rule. Long, long, long ago, kids couldn't go to schools together or sit on the bus together if they had different color eyes. Martin made them change that crazy law."

I didn't tell her about her mistake.

I told her the truth.

I told her I thought it was perfect and that I thought
Ms. Amara would love it and that if he could read it, Martin the
King would love it, too.

—

January 21, Thursday

I love:

$$3 \times 8 = 24$$

I am in the fours group, finally!!!

So is Xavier. I guess we did learn something, in between
getting smooshed into goo by his big brother.

Gianni Schicci is not in the fours group. He is the only one
left in threes.

I no thank you:

Student council

Staying for after-school violin

—

January 22, Friday

The club that has no boys in it had a party today at lunch.
They all brought in bags of pretzels and popcorn, and they
shared. Also they whispered. And giggled.

The boys all sat kind of glum eating our own lunches.

Suddenly, Gianni Schicci punched me hard in the arm and asked, "Don't you hate girls?"

The true thing I was thinking was: *No, I hate people who punch me hard in the arm.* But I thought that might get me punched more. It takes a brave person to stand up to a bully and tell the truth; we had just learned that this morning in our No Bullies Allowed assembly.

But I am not a brave person.

So I said, "Yeah."

"I love girls," Noah said with his mouth full of tuna fish.

"You *are* a girl," Gianni said, and giggled. It wasn't a happy giggle like the girls' giggles, though.

"No," said Noah. "I'm a boy." Noah is not so good at recognizing sarcasm, I think. Or maybe he is a brave person.

———

January 23, Saturday

The good thing about basketball:

    No dogs allowed in the gym

The bad thing about basketball:

    Everything else

———

January 24, Sunday

The other good thing about basketball:

Nobody expects you to practice it on days you don't

have it even if you stink

Unlike violin.

January 25, Monday

Noah tried to play with the girls at lunch. They didn't let him.

Then he tried to play with the boys. Gianni and Xavier said

he couldn't, because we were playing Savers of the Universe and

that's only for boys. Noah tried the "I'm a boy" argument, and

then he tried the "Actually, the girls sometimes play Savers of

the Universe, too" argument.

Apparently neither one was convincing.

So Noah slunk off by himself to sit on a rock.

Nobody went to sit with him because you really don't want to get on the bad side of Xavier Schwartz and Gianni Schicci.

Noah looked really sad.

I couldn't stand it.

So I did the probably stupidest thing I ever did in my life, which is kind of an accomplishment from a kid who suggested Rarest Pus as a class theme and also convinced his parents to buy a dog when he is absolutely terrified of dogs, so now he can't ever sit in his own living room or anywhere in his house except his top bunk bed, which also terrifies him.

I went and sat on the rock with Noah.

—

January 26, Tuesday

I was right.

It was definitely my stupidest move ever.

I may as well let Qwerty gobble me up. At least I wouldn't have to go back to school tomorrow and have another day like today.

—

January 27, Wednesday

Today was Montana C.'s birthday. Her mom came in with a cake and we all sang. Ms. Termini even smiled at her and gave her an extra Superstar.

Then Ms. Termini took out her hippopotamus puppet and made Montana C. sit on a stool in the front of the class, and each of us had to say why we were happy that Montana C. had been born.

The first time Ms. Termini did that tradition, back in September for Montana B.'s birthday, we were all totally freaked out. By now we are used to it.

Here are some things people said:

I'm glad Montana C. was born because she is very smart and always willing to help other people understand stuff. (That was from a girl named Willow.)

I'm glad Montana C. was born because she's fast, so our team won in gym. (That was Xavier Schwartz.)

I'm glad Montana C. was born because she's fun. (That was me. And then I almost threw up.)

At lunch Montana C. let me and Noah play with her and Daisy.

January 28, Thursday

Now Xavier Schwartz and Gianni Schicci hate me more than ever.

They said Montana C. is my girlfriend.

I didn't even bother pointing out that you can't have a girlfriend in third grade.

I just went to student council and voted that yes there should be Pajama Day in April. Why not? It's not like things could get worse.

—

January 29, Friday

It snowed!

And, after they gave us the usual boring speech about how we're not allowed to throw snowballs except against the wall, someone could get hurt, blah blah blah, they let us have an extra-long recess to play in it! The third and fourth graders all got to go out on the lower playground for a full hour.

At first we were all just running around like lunatics. But soon people started making snowballs. Noah said to me, "Uh-oh. This could get ugly."

I nodded. Some of those fourth graders are pretty huge. And they were grabbing chunks of ice.

Noah and I stayed as far away from them as we could. We were throwing snowballs at the wall like we were supposed to, but Noah is even worse at throwing than I am. One of his hit a fourth grader named Thor on the leg.

Suddenly a gang of huge fourth graders were chasing us with their ice balls, and Thor pitched one right into Noah's head. Noah fell smashing down to the ground.

Every third grader crowded around Noah to see if he was okay and scream at the fourth-grade bullies. Daisy walked Noah to the nurse while Xavier Schwartz, Gianni Schicci, Montana C., and I pelted those jerks with as many snowballs as we could.

January 30, Saturday

Dad had a talk with me on our way to basketball, about

getting sent to the principal for the second time in my life.

He said he was proud of me for standing up for my friend.

I just said thanks but I was proud, too. We all were, I could tell, from how me and Montana C. and Xavier Schwartz and Gianni Schicci were all smiling at each other while we sat in the bad-kid chairs outside the principal's office.

We should have used our words, the principal said. He did say we were good not to use ice balls in revenge, and that the fourth graders were in much bigger trouble.

Afterward, Xavier Schwartz whispered to me, "Words are good but snowballs are better."

—

January 31, Sunday

Gingy and Poopsie came over for dinner.

Mom made me play my violin for them.

They looked like it hurt their teeth.

But afterward Poopsie gave me a dollar. For the concert, he said.

I think it was really for playing only two songs instead of all five.

—

February 1, Monday

A good thing about basketball:

It is not push-ups

I no thank you gym class. Push-ups are ridiculous. It is just relaxing, interrupted, over and over again.

—

February 2, Tuesday

Valentine's Day is coming early this year. That sounds impossible but it is not. Valentine's Day this year is on a Sunday, and it is the Sunday at the beginning of winter break. So we are doing Valentine's Day celebrations on February 12.

Ten days.

The bad news: no store-boughts allowed in Ms. Termini's class, and no candy, even if it is from your own candy store.

The worse news: You have to make one for every kid in the whole darn class. Plus, because she is Ms. Termini, there is homework about it. The valentines can't just say "Happy V-Day. From, Justin." We have to write the person's name in our best cursive writing on an index card and then, still in our best cursive writing, write a compliment that is true but also nice.

One compliment for every kid in the class.

There are some kids I am going to have a real challenge with.

124

And not just because we didn't learn how to do *X*s in cursive yet.

—

February 3, Wednesday

I walked the dog.

I totally walked the dog.

Well, I mean, Mom held the leash most of the time. But I held it with her for a while, and even when Qwerty yanked, I didn't fall down and I didn't cry.

Mom said, "See? Not so bad, huh, Justin?"

But her eyes said "proud."

February 4, Thursday

Noah wants to buy chocolates for Ms. Burns for Valentine's Day. He has over 11 dollars saved up. He could buy a medium red heart with truffles if he borrows three more dollars from me.

I am not being greedy. I honestly think it is a bad idea.

For so many reasons.

Not just because of what Xavier Schwartz and Gianni Schicci would say about him.

———

February 5, Friday

I got into the sevens of times tables. That is the highest group. Also I got a Superstar for moving up so fast. It was not that hard. The only hard one for me was $3 \times 8 = 24$, and I will never forget that one as long as I live.

And even $3 \times 8 = 24$ was not the hard part. It was being asked it with everybody looking at me, imagining how I would feel if I messed up, and then realizing that while I was imagining messing up, I was not answering, and then it was too late. Slow is the same as a mess-up in times tables.

What I needed was a trick for not thinking of messing up. Once I worked out the trick, it was smooth sailing for me and times tables.

This is my trick:

Speed.

I go over my flash cards of the times tables I'm up to so many times in my bed that the answer comes as fast as the second syllable of my name. I can't *not* say it. So 24 comes after 3×8 as fast as Tin after Jus. I don't have to think at all.

Maybe that's a dumb trick but it works for me.

—

February 6, Saturday

I think my finger is broken.

It is at least jammed.

Gianni Schicci threw the basketball so hard at me when all I was doing was running to get out of the way. If I'd wanted him to throw it to me for some reason, I would have said, "Here!" Did anybody hear me yell "Here!" on the basketball court?

Ever?

Noah sat with his arm around me on the bench while I held the melting ice on my finger, and the tears inside my eyes. He only jumped up to cheer when we won. For a kid who has no interest in sports, Noah is sure an enthusiastic cheerer.

—

February 7, Sunday

It's not broken.

It didn't even manage a decent bruise.

So frustrating.

Because nobody believes me that I can't write the compliments now. A finger can be badly hurt without a bruise.

Five kids down, seventeen more compliments to go.

And speaking of compliments, I walked Qwerty all by myself. Dad came along, but I held the leash by myself. And I threw Qwerty a cookie, too.

I only freaked out a little.

I think I deserved a little more of a compliment than I got for all that.

February 8, Monday

Elizabeth bought valentines. She is deciding who will get the cutest one. She has three boyfriends now.

Mom told her there is no such thing as boyfriends or girlfriends in elementary school. Just friends.

Elizabeth smiled her angel smile and said, "I know that, Mommy, but I have three boyfriends anyway."

I told her I thought Buckey was her boyfriend and that she was planning to marry him.

She looked at me with a pity face and explained with a patient sigh that she was younger when she said that, and for now she is keeping her options open.

Mom and I cracked up about that the rest of the night.

—

February 9, Tuesday

Nobody told me anything about a violin recital.

Dad said my least favorite thing after *hurry*, which is "calm down, Justin, calm down."

But he is not the one who doesn't know how to hold the bow right or get the violin to do anything other than scream in pain, and then be forced to torture an innocent musical instrument in front of the whole world, is he?

And he is also not the one who has to think of a true but nice compliment for Gianni Schicci and one for Xavier Schwartz, too.

He thinks running a candy store just before Valentine's Day is stressful? He should try third grade just before Valentine's Day.

—

February 10, Wednesday

Well, it's not great, but here is what I came up with:

Gianni has a way of finding the humor in situations where other people might not find any.

Xavier is very strong for his size and sees more in people than they see in themselves.

At least I'm done.

—

February 11, Thursday

It is hard to think about anything except Valentine's Day. Especially because it is the busiest time of year at our store.

But also because I keep wondering:

What will people say about me?

—

February 12, Friday

Here are my favorite Valentine's notes that I got:

1. Montana B.: Justin is nice because he is not mean.

2. Willow: Justin is a boy who is funny without using bathroom words.

3. Bartholomew Wiggins: I think Justin K. has a good heart, an original way of thinking about things, and more imaginative creativity than he lets most people see.

4. Gianni Schicci: Justin Case is the funniest boy in third grade. Rarest Pus rules!

5. Carlos: I like Justin because he is frecklier than me.

6. Montana C.: Justin K. is a good person who stands up for his friends and little sister, makes people feel happy, and is also a fast runner.

7. Penelope Ann Murphy: Justin waited with me once when I had a bloody nose in kindergarten at the nurse's office. I will never forget his niceness and that he has never teased me about it even though I cried.

8. Xavier Schwartz: If you ever were in a bad mess, the kid you would want by your side is Justin Case.

—

February 13, Saturday

I keep reading my valentines over and over.

—

February 14, Sunday

Busiest day of the year at our store.

If I never see another shiny red heart or another chocolate truffle, that is just fine with me.

Mom gave Dad his traditional Valentine's gift of socks, and he gave her a Swiss Army knife and also two red velvet pillows that she put right on the corners of the couch, and they both giggled. (Mom and Dad. Not the pillows.)

They are kind of weird, I am starting to think. (Mom and Dad again. The pillows are just couch pillows, although red.)

Daisy and her dad came into the store to buy candies for her mom. Daisy didn't really talk to me while they were ordering but before they left she whispered, "Happy Valentine's Day." I said, "You, too." Her big brother came in later, by himself, and bought a small, red, shiny heart box with a bow on it and caramels inside. His face was red, too, and he kept looking at his sneakers. Xavier Schwartz's big brother came in about half an hour later and bought the same heart.

I thought, *What if they give them to each other?* That would be funny.

If not, what if they both gave them to a girl, and it turned out to be the same girl? So then I started wondering which of those big gawky boys that girl would choose as her valentine. Also I wonder if I will ever look at my sneakers and buy a shiny red heart box full of candy for a girl when I am a teenager, and which girl would I do that for?

Probably I won't.

If I bought a big box of candy with my own money, I might share it, but I would definitely want to keep some candy, plus the box, for myself.

132

And then Dad said, "Justin! Justin! Earth to Justin!" when I was just thinking about the future for one minute.

—

February 15, Monday

Hooray for vacation!

The dog already got taken to the kennel and our house is weirdly quiet. Was it always this quiet before we got him? I can't decide if I love it or not so much. But I have no more time for that because I have to find my goggles or I won't be able to swim in the pool in Florida at all.

I hope there are movies on the plane.

Also I hope the plane doesn't fall out of the sky.

Oh, great.

Why did I have to even think of that?

I will try to worry about there being a bad movie on the plane. Sometimes a little worry can crowd out a big worry.

Now I am worrying about what to worry about.

—

February 16, Tuesday

The plane stayed in the sky the whole time it needed to, which has to do with physics and lift. Dad explained it to me but I still don't fully get it.

What I should have worried about instead of crashing was the surprise Mom kept hinting about. I thought it was going to be something like gummy bears.

It wasn't.

It was nothing gummy.

Unless you count Buckey. He is kind of gummy.

And he was in the seat next to Elizabeth on the plane that stayed in the air. Which meant that next to me was Montana C.

Because our families are such good friends, apparently, we had planned our vacation together.

I was not consulted, obviously.

And I was not sulking in the hotel room, either. I was drawing pictures of Wobble-butt, who I made up while I wasn't sulking on the plane, and who has magical powers.

—

February 17, Wednesday

Montana C. saw me doodling Wobble-butt on the paper tablecloth.

134

I thought she was going to be like, *Ew, you have an imaginary friend? You should go play with Elizabeth and Buckey.*

Wobble-butt!

But she didn't. She said, "Who's that?" and then she cracked up at his name and asked me to teach her how to draw him, so I did. And we made up a bunch of adventures Wobble-butt gets into.

Montana C. has a retainer for her crooked teeth that she hides under a teacup while she eats. (The retainer goes under the teacup, not her crooked teeth. That would be really weird.)

She said thanks for not thinking the retainer was gross, but I honestly thought it was awesome. It looked so disgusting.

Then we went down to the beach and we kept talking about Wobble-butt, and if maybe he is a superhero.

———

February 18, Thursday

Dad went to the store to buy us some stuff. Mom gave him

a list. It had sunblock and bug spray on it but also, because we begged, cookies. Montana C.'s family has so much junk and we have nothing but a few granola bars. So Mom said okay. She gets very relaxed from the sound of waves.

We should not have sent that man to the store on his own.

The kind of cookies he bought were called Jaffa Cakes. According to the package, Jaffa Cakes have orange-centered yippie and also a squidgy bit. They are from England.

Apparently British children are weird.

February 19, Friday

Mom says it was from sunburn, but I know it was actually Jaffa Man.

I heard him come into our hotel room last night. I know it was him because he was making squidgy noises. Then I heard a very growly voice muttering, "Yippie. Yippie. Yippie."

It is tough luck that I woke everybody up by turning on the light.

I think he was coming to get those darn Jaffa Cakes.

Which he can totally have.

I don't even know what they really are.

February 20, Saturday

Elizabeth told Montana C. that I had a nightmare because of cookies.

"Cookies?" Montana C. asked. "You had a nightmare about . . . cookies?"

"They aren't cookies!" I yelled.

"Well, what are they?" she asked.

"They are Jaffa Cakes!"

We just stared at each other for a while at that.

Then she asked, "What's a Jaffa Cake?"

"It is a dessert from England," I said, trying not to yell, "that my dad bought instead of normal cookies. They have a squidgy bit."

"A squidgy bit?"

"Yes!" I said, kind of yelling. "And an orange-centered yippie!"

Montana C. backed up two steps. "Okay, now I'm afraid of it, too."

"I am not afraid of it," I yelled.

"But Elizabeth said . . ."

"I'm not!" I yelled. "I am only afraid of Jaffa Man!"

"Jaffa Man?" she yelled. "Jaffa Man is Wobble-butt's archenemy!"

Which made me totally "thank you" Montana C.

—

February 21, Sunday

The best part of vacation wasn't learning to boogie board, or cannonballing into the pool, or getting to go in the hot tub unlike kindergartners, or even the traps we made to catch Jaffa Man that ended up catching Elizabeth and Buckey instead (a total accident, I swear).

It was not even getting the ice from the ice machine.

It was when Montana C. lost her retainer at lunch today.

We were on our way back to the beach to check our Jaffa traps (with the squidgy bits at the bottom) when Montana C. slapped her hand over her mouth.

"What?" I asked.

"My retainer!" she yelled. "I left it . . ."

"Under the teacup?"

We zoomed straight to the restaurant. She got there first and yanked open the door. Just as the blast of air-conditioning hit us, we heard an old lady shriek.

We zigzagged to the table. Two old ladies were slanted back from the table, their faces stretched long, their hands up in the air like the retainer might jump off the saucer and bite them.

Montana C. reached past the one holding the teacup up, plucked the retainer off the saucer, and whispered quickly, "Sorry, thank you, that's my squidgy bit, sorry."

She popped the retainer into her mouth and clicked it into place with her tongue. The two ladies were blinking furiously, moving their mouths in search of some angry words to yell, but Montana C. and I are the two fastest kids in the whole third grade of W. H. Taft Elementary School, so we were out the door and cannonballing into the deep end and screaming "Orange-centered YIPPIE!" before they found a single nasty word.

February 22, Monday

Back to school!

Montana C. clicked her retainer during morning meeting and

I had to go sit in the library corner until I could contain myself.

I never knew how hard I was to contain.

—

February 23, Tuesday

What I am good at:

Math

Video games

Worrying

What I am bad at:

Push-ups

Violin

Being brave

Walking Qwerty, which is my responsibility on

Wednesdays and Saturday mornings

Containing myself when somebody says the word *squidgy*

—

February 24, Wednesday

We had a big grade-wide meeting today. There is a new thing in our school for third graders and we are the first year it is happening to. That's because Ms. Burns brought it from her old school, which was in New York City.

The big thing is called Dinosaur Day.

Each student has to do a research paper and a project about the dinosaur subject of our choice. (No groups, hallelujah.)

My idea, which I thought of right away, is to build a model of a stegosaurus (my favorite dinosaur, because of the stegs) and a model of a human, so you can see the differences between the circulatory systems, the digestive systems, the skeletal systems, everything. I think that will be a great project. Ms. Burns is the person in charge of Dinosaur Day, which will be next month and all the parents will come for it.

Ms. Burns said, "Think big. Be ambitious." Then she winked.

Maybe I could also do a T. rex.

—

February 25, Thursday

Yesterday I asked Mom to come with me for my walking of Qwerty, and the reason was not because I am lazy or scared; it was because I wanted to tell her my great idea for Dinosaur

Day. So eventually she stopped doing her million things she was frantically doing and came. I was thinking she would say she was so proud of me for having an interesting mind and thinking big.

What she said instead was no.

When I tried to explain why it was a good idea, she said, "Talk to your father about it. I am done parenting for the day."

But when I tried to talk to them both about it again tonight and explain my big idea, they couldn't listen to it because they were very busy watching Elizabeth practice her ballet routine for her ballet recital. Her ballet class is performing *Cinderella*. All the girls in her ballet class wanted to be Cinderella. So they all are. The teacher is playing all the other parts. The name of the show is going to be "The Twelve Cinderellas."

Ballet is apparently much more important than homework in our family these days.

—

February 26, Friday

We had to hand in our plans for Dinosaur Day projects.

I had nothing else to write down, because of the "Twelve Cinderellas" issue.

So that is why I had to write down that I am planning to create scale models of the stegosaurus and the human being to show how they are similar and different. I left out the T. rex because there are limits.

Now it is too late to change it, because I wrote it down and handed it in. That is a thing Poopsie says is called "facts on the ground."

But I have a little bad feeling in my stomach, because of that "no" Mom said to my idea when I mentioned it, and then writing it anyway.

—

February 27, Saturday

I didn't say anything to Mom and Dad about the whole Dinosaur Day problem. I figured we would jump off that bridge when we come to it.

I didn't want to tell Mom and Dad not just because I didn't want to get in trouble, but also because they were already having a hard enough day dealing with me. They were pretty fed up from all my moping about having to walk Qwerty (which Dad eventually did instead), and then play basketball, and then sit through "The Twelve Cinderellas," and then go out to dinner with Gingy and Poopsie, who brought flowers for "the best Cinderella," who wore her tutu on her head all through dinner at the Chinese restaurant with the fish tank. Which smells funky.

So they'd had enough trouble from me already. No need to pile more on them.

—

February 28, Sunday

I had to tell somebody, though.

So I told Wingnut.

He may not be real, but he is an excellent listener. He thinks it will turn out okay. He doesn't think I will get in trouble for promising to make a scale model of a stegosaurus and a human being. Even though I actually have no idea how to make a scale model. And I don't know anything really about the skeletal or digestive or muscular systems of a stegosaurus or a human being. And I promised to do something my parents both said I was not allowed to promise.

Wingnut is confident it will all work out fine.

Wingnut is very loving.

But maybe not the smartest stuffty on the bed.

—

March 1, Monday

I got a "see me" on my Dinosaur Day proposal.

And for the sixth month in a row, I did not win the Superstar competition. This month it was Bartholomew Wiggins.

He is the only boy who has ever won. He also got a "great idea!" on his Dinosaur Day proposal, I happened to see.

I am starting to no thank you Bartholomew Wiggins.

—

March 2, Tuesday

I wasn't in trouble. And the "me" I had to see turned out to be Ms. Burns. I had to go have a conference at her desk.

She was "impressed" with my "ambition." (Seriously, she said those exact words.) But she thought maybe I could choose a system in each of the stegosaurus and the human being to do a comparison with.

My head kept nodding. It was a good suggestion, that's why.

Then I was allowed to go down to lunch. All the boys gathered around me to find out what I had done wrong to have to stay in and get talked to.

145

I told them, "Nothing."

They all kind of did the bobble-head thing of "oh, okay, whatever."

I think they thought I had gotten in trouble and was just embarrassed about it. We had recess in the gym, after, because of the rain, and Xavier Schwartz picked me second for dodgeball.

If I actually had gotten in trouble, getting picked second for dodgeball by Xavier Schwartz really might have cheered me up. Too bad I was already cheered. Because of having impressive ambition and also because I didn't have to get in trouble with Mom and Dad anymore. But I will try to save the cheered feeling for when I need it.

—

March 3, Wednesday

What I wish:

That I could speed-read all these boring books about dinosaurs

That I could be brave about walking Qwerty and the Way-Back of the basement (and even The Boiler) and everything else

That I didn't have violin or basketball

That I could have flying and invisibility powers

That I still had playdates with Daisy

Although maybe not so much on that last one. I had a good time doing LEGOS and videos with Noah today.

I am not even sure what Daisy likes to play anymore.

But invisibility would be cool.

—

March 4, Thursday

I can't find Wingnut.

—

March 5, Friday

Still no sign of Wingnut.

I have never lost him for so long before.

Stegosauruses have brains the size of walnuts. People have brains the size of their two fists combined.

But my big fat brain cannot remember where I had Wingnut last, no matter how much I try.

—

March 6, Saturday

Last day of basketball.

My team was in last place but we got trophies anyway. Uncle Jon came over for dinner, and after he walked Qwerty for/with me, he admired all my trophies. He said I must be a really excellent athlete.

I told him I truly am not.

He argued that only a great athlete could get so many trophies. He played Little League for, like, ten years and he only got one trophy in his life, and that was at a friend's bowling birthday party when everybody got one. I tried to explain that they just give trophies out to all the kids now at the end of every season, no matter what.

I don't think he was listening. He likes the idea of having a jock nephew, I guess, and he really didn't want me to wreck that for him.

Still no sign of Wingnut.

—

March 7, Sunday

Snakey looks awfully suspicious.

Bananas is questioning all the stuffties on the bed about when they last saw Wingnut.

Nobody said anything to me but I think I heard somebody

in the back corner of the bed, where the rough stuffties hang out, whisper the name of Bad Boy.

March 8, Monday

So I am doing the Human Brain and Spinal Cord versus the Stegosaurus Brain and Spinal Cord.

I don't even care.

Noah sat with me at lunch. I told him about Wingnut. He didn't talk or try to cheer me up. He didn't say, *Well, where did you last play with him?* And he especially didn't say anything like, *You still play with stuffed animals?* even though he doesn't anymore.

He just sat there with me all through lunch and recess, just sat there by my side.

March 9, Tuesday

What I wish I could invent:

A magical finder and you could whisper into it what you need it to find and then *poof*! The thing would be right there in your arms (or, if it was too big, like if you lost your car or grandfather, it could just appear in a convenient but obvious place). And the thing that was lost would be not good as new, which would be weird in the case of a grandfather or a stuffty that you love most in the world, but just like they were when you last saw the thing or person or whatever.

But I don't know how to invent a magic finder.

And instead of trying to figure out how to invent one, I have to go make horrible noises on my violin.

—

March 10, Wednesday

I got a Superstar for being quiet.

I am always quiet. Well, almost always. If I got a Superstar every time I was quiet this year, I would have a whole constellation of Superstars. I would be the total Superstar champion.

Gianni Schicci asked why I am so frowny lately. I said I had lost my favorite stuffed animal. He said, "You don't still play with stuffed animals, do you?" So I had to say, "No, of course not." He turned a little red and quickly said, "No, me neither."

Then he walked away fast.

Well, at least he didn't mock me. I might have had to knock him down if he did; that's how sad and angry I am at this whole thing. I don't even care if I get sent to the principal's office.

Instead of taking Qwerty for a walk, I let him out the back door. He was perfectly happy, but I got in trouble anyway. He could get hit by a car or run away. It was very irresponsible of me. They expect more from me.

Only Qwerty likes me in my family, and I wish he would not like me quite so much, or so droolily.

—

March 11, Thursday

I got called out of student council to go to the nurse's office, because, the teacher said, my sister was there and needed me. On my way there, I was going over and over Mom's and Dad's cell phone numbers, just in case they had to be called to come to school or the hospital. I was picturing riding in an ambulance with Elizabeth, and in my imagination I was very brave and not freaking out at all. I told myself to pretend to be brave once I got there, even if I wasn't really, and that that kind of faking is not the same as lying. Elizabeth would need me to be calm and strong, I told myself, so that is what I would pretend to be.

When I got to the nurse's office, Elizabeth was sitting nicely in a chair, waiting for me. She wasn't bleeding or puking or panicking or dying in any visible way.

We said hi to each other and then I looked at the nurse, who explained that Elizabeth had a loose tooth that had bled a little tiny drop ("a lot," Elizabeth interrupted) and that the blood had freaked Elizabeth out. She had apparently told the nurse she'd feel better if she could just get a hug from me, and that's why the nurse sent for me.

"Oh," I said.

I hugged Elizabeth. She hugged me back tight. Then she showed me her slightly wiggly tooth, I said, "cool," and then I walked her back to her class.

She held my hand and smiled the whole way.

—

March 12, Friday

We had to hand in our final project ideas for Dinosaur Day.

Mine stinks.

It is:

I will show the difference between the brain and spinal cord of a human being and of a stegosaurus. I will measure my spinal cord and cut string that length, then attach it to a balloon the size of my two fists/brain. I will also cut 60 feet of string for the right length of a steg spinal cord, and attach it to a walnut.

I wrote that down and handed it in.

It occurs to me that if I fail out of third grade, I will have to do the year over. Which would really stink. Eventually I could end up 37 years old and still a third grader.

I'd probably rock at dodgeball by then, though.

—

March 13, Saturday

Little League?

Could we get a week off, for goodness' sake?

—

March 14, Sunday

Elizabeth lost her tooth.

I mean she really, fully lost it.

It was bleeding a little this morning and I guess Elizabeth really is allergic to the taste of blood because it made her throw up. Right into the kitchen sink. Luckily we have a garbage disposal so after she finished, Mom ran the water and turned on the garbage disposal to get rid of it. I had run out into the living room because puking is high on my list of no thank you activities to witness.

Elizabeth came and sat down next to me on the couch. Qwerty trotted after her and put his head on Elizabeth's lap. Elizabeth tried to convince me to let Qwerty at least smell my hand. I didn't want to explain, again, that the dog's huge teeth are about an inch from his wet nose, so thanks anyway. So I just said I wasn't in the mood.

Elizabeth thought it was not that I was scared of Qwerty but that I was feeling sad again about Wingnut, so she smiled all loving at me and said she was sure I would find Wingnut really soon.

I almost cried at that, not because she was right or wrong or because it was so nice of her to try to reassure me, but because I had for that one moment forgotten to feel sad about Wingnut. Which made me feel SO guilty, like now maybe

Wingnut would never come back to me. But I didn't cry, because I got distracted — by the huge hole in Elizabeth's mouth.

"What happened to your tooth?" I asked her.

"Nothing," she said, and then touched the place with her tongue, and made a weird possibly-about-to-puke-again noise inside her throat.

"It fell out?" I asked her.

She nodded, turning green.

"When?"

She shrugged.

"Maybe while you were puking!"

We both ran into the kitchen and dared each other to put our hands down the garbage disposal to feel around for the tooth, which, even if we were allowed to do such a dangerous thing and Mom wouldn't kill us or our hands wouldn't get grinded off, I still no way would do it, especially to dig through the puke.

We screamed for Mom but she wouldn't do it, either.

—

March 15, Monday

Mom used the garbage disposal this morning after breakfast.

I thought Elizabeth was going to shatter every window in the house with her screaming.

She didn't even care about the golden dollar she got from the tooth fairy. Though she did thank me for writing the tooth fairy a note explaining the fully lost tooth situation.

I hardly slept all night, on the lookout in case an actual fairy really came to our house and was a nasty one.

—

March 16, Tuesday

Gianni Schicci cheats.

He said he didn't get tagged in Lawyers in the Underworld but he totally did, and then he quit and went to hang out by the fence. Noah and I were kind of the leaders of Lawyers in the Underworld because we invented it, and we were explaining to the other kids about you have a secret spot of weakness and if you can get through the third level of Underworld Trials without a ghoul using a power (like fire, or spit, depending on the ghoul) against you, you'd go up to the ghost level of peril. But in the middle, Gianni started screaming that he had found Witchie Poo.

So we of course all had to run and check it out.

It really did look like Witchie Poo. Montana C. laughed and said it was just dog poo. She and Xavier and I weren't scared. Daisy looked a little unsure. (Like I felt.)

Then Gianni got the idea of touching the poo that might have been Witchie Poo with a stick and chasing everybody with it.

I ran away fast because I don't honestly care what kind of poo it was on that stick; I still would prefer not to be touched with it.

March 17, Wednesday

It's Saint Patrick's Day. Also Gingy's birthday. (Also my day to walk Qwerty, which I got Poopsie to do with me.)

We are not Irish but we all wear green for Gingy's birthday in my family, because green is her favorite color and when she was a little girl she always thought everybody wore green on her birthday in her honor.

Except every year when she tells us that story when we go out to dinner for her birthday, she doesn't say, "When I was a little girl." She says, "When I was a girl."

And every year I wonder if she means that now she is a boy.

Which she definitely is not.

—

March 18, Thursday

We had time in school to work on our Dinosaur Day project.

Gianni Schicci kept trying to look at my paper.

I didn't let him. It's not that I was scared of getting caught.

He should do his own work.

Also, he should not chase people with poo on a stick.

Or say he wasn't tagged when he totally was.

—

March 19, Friday

Noah is sick. He hasn't been in school since Tuesday. There

is a rumor that he got witchie sickness from the Witchie Poo. Nobody really believes it but I called him when I got home from school just in case.

He has bronchitis, not witchie sickness. But he is feeling better. That's good because his birthday party is tomorrow, and it would be weird to have it without him.

———

March 20, Saturday

Noah didn't have to go to Little League because of getting over bronchitis. He didn't miss much. We lost, 3–1. I struck out all three times I was up, though Dad said I had good swings — now it's just about connecting with the ball. That one little element of the thing is all that's messing me up, apparently. That would be a problem mitt-wise, too, since balls generally don't connect with my mitt any more than they do with my bat, but I solve that by going as far out as possible into left field and making sure Gianni Schicci is in front of me. Luckily Gianni is a total ball hog.

Baseball is my favorite sport. It's much more relaxing than my other sports. (Or walking Qwerty, which I did by myself today but only got just past the driveway before I felt like my heart might burst, so we went back.)

After the game we went straight to Noah's party, which was at a paint-on-pottery place. It was the first party of the year where girls and boys were both invited.

I ended up sitting next to Daisy. We didn't talk to each other.

Well, at the end I said her unicorn was really good. And she whispered that she liked how I painted my bear.

I almost told her about losing Wingnut, but the cake came out and it was time to sing so I didn't.

—

March 21, Sunday

It's the first day of spring, and it is freezing cold and raining out.

Nobody has slept on the Pillow of Honor for a long time. I am keeping it clear just in case Wingnut finds his way back to the bed when I am not looking.

—

March 22, Monday

Dinosaur Day is Friday and we are very far from ready. We have to hand in our final drafts of our research papers by tomorrow.

I wish I had chosen a dinosaur with a shorter name than stegosaurus. Like T. rex.

Maybe I could just write "steg" so my hand doesn't fall the heck off.

—

March 23, Tuesday

Well, I handed it in, my final draft. I think I did okay. Some of the stuff I read (and wrote) did not make a lot of sense to me (like stuff about genus, which is not at all the same as genius, and a lot of words in Greek, which I don't speak).

I liked that *stegosaurus* means "roof lizard" so I included that even though it is not strictly about its brain.

They could have called it "bus lizard" because it was the size and weight of a bus, even though its brain weighed less than half as much as the yogurt I took for lunch today.

So I ate more than two steg brain's worth of yogurt today. Ew.

Maybe tomorrow I'll bring a sandwich.

—

March 24, Wednesday

Xavier Schwartz came for a playdate.

I let him hold Qwerty's leash when we walked him.

Xavier wishes he had Qwerty as a pet.

Me too.

Except for the fact that Bad Boy hasn't been around since Qwerty moved in with us. As far as I know.

But still.

Anyway, Mom said no, Xavier could take home a cookie but not our dog.

Other than that it was not a terrible playdate. And now we have reciprocated, which is what Mom said we at least had to do, so maybe I don't have to play with Xavier Schwartz again until fourth grade. If ever.

—

March 25, Thursday

Everybody pitched in to help with the Dinosaur Day project. Instead of just a balloon the size of my brain, we made a papier-mâché brain on top of the balloon. Elizabeth tore newspapers into strips, Mom and Dad dipped them in the glunky paste, and I smoothed the strips onto the balloon. It was gross but cool. While that was drying, Dad measured my spine and we cut a string that size (15 inches) and then measured out the 60 feet for the steg's spinal cord, and Krazy Glued one end to a walnut. Mom had to buy a whole bag of them just so I could have one.

"Anybody want a walnut?" she asked, holding the full-except-one-walnut bag.

"Justin should put them in a basket to give them out to everybody at Dinosaur Day," Elizabeth suggested.

"Why would I give out walnuts?" I asked. I admit I was a little cranky because even though my project was okay, it wasn't great. Noah had made a T. rex head out of a football helmet and his parents bought a Polaroid camera to take pictures of each kid wearing it and you get to bring the picture home. Or, from me, they could have, hooray, a nut.

"You could make a sign and attach it to the basket and the sign would say, 'Free Stegosaurus Brains!'"

Which I had to admit, even though she was in kindergarten, was a totally awesome idea.

—

March 26, Friday

Dinosaur Day was excellent.

We set the whole thing up in the auditorium and all the grades came. The projects were so cool: Montana C. made dinosaur footprints in clay and you could measure yours against them, and Noah's was great with the T. rex helmet, and Xavier Schwartz made a card game that should totally be a real thing in stores, with all the dinosaurs and their attack powers and defense powers and you try to demolish each other. Daisy did a diorama of an oviraptor trying to steal eggs and a mom dinosaur fighting him off. She is very artistic. (Daisy, not the mom dinosaur.)

Bartholomew Wiggins did something to do with apatosaurus DNA, which I didn't really get, but it filled up a huge opening-poster-board thing. And he dressed up as a paleontologist, which was pretty funny.

But what a lot of people kept saying, all day long, was, "Check out my steg brain! Go get a steg brain — free — from that kid with the curly hair over there!"

Even Ms. Termini and Ms. Burns took steg brains.

That felt really, really good.

March 27, Saturday

Before Little League, Dad and I did extra pop-up practice.

Dad said when he was a kid he always used to imagine playing center field for the Yankees. He asked if I ever imagine doing that.

I shook my head. I said sometimes I imagine I am in a bakery.

Dad didn't seem so impressed with that imagining.

—

March 28, Sunday

Today we cooked. We're going to celebrate Passover tomorrow night at my cousins' house.

Awesome. Can't wait.

And then the fun will continue. Because guess where we are going for vacation! Disney World? LEGOLAND? Australia?

Wrong.

Mom and Dad have to work. So we are going to have a "staycation," which means stay home and do a big fat nothing over vacation, and Gingy and Poopsie are going to come and take care of us and feed us food that jiggles, probably.

—

March 29, Monday

I do not have a bad attitude.

I have car sickness.

The New Jersey Turnpike should be called the New Jersey Parking Lot. The only thing that cheered me up about being on it was not being at my cousins' house yet.

—

March 30, Tuesday

Sometimes things turn out better than you think they will.

I was all, *What if I have to ask the Four Questions* and *What if my cousins slime me again* and *Maybe we should have brought flashlights just in case there is a blackout in the middle of the night while we're there and we can't find our way around and we have to pee.*

But none of that happened.

It was actually fun. My cousins metamorphosized into human beings and also they got a new game system that we were allowed to play before the Passover Seder. Then at the Seder we did a lot of singing and the grown-ups drank wine and

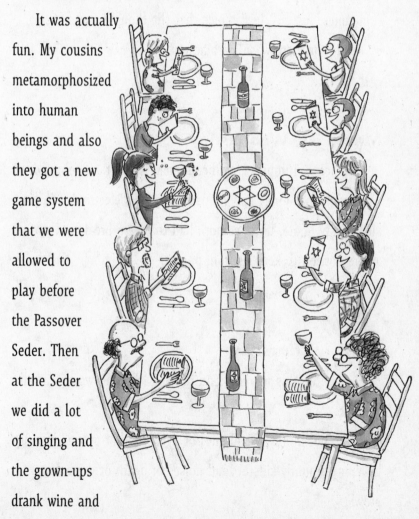

we drank grape juice and the only person who spilled was Mom.

My cousins asked the Four Questions. I was the oldest kid at the table. Elizabeth said the four sons in the Passover story were like the four of us: I was the wise one, she was the wicked one, Dermot was the dim-witted one, and Dylan was the baby. I told her she wasn't wicked and she said, "You know I am sometimes, Justin." It was nice that she thought I was wise.

And that there wasn't a blackout.

—

March 31, Wednesday

The Jersey Turnpike is no better going south than going north.

Except that Gingy and Poopsie bought us electronics to play all the way home, until we both had to take a break and stare at the horizon to keep us from puking.

—

April 1, Thursday

I woke up this morning and realized I had no worries at all anymore.

I am not afraid of bad guys or jiggly food or getting beat up by runny-aroundy kids or loud noises or death or dogs that growl.

168

I have become the bravest kid in the world.

April Fools.

—

April 2, Friday

Mom and Dad think we can't hear when they are fighting but we can.

Elizabeth came into my room way after lights-out when we were supposed to be sleeping and Mom and Dad were going over their papers. They were working on their taxes and they kept not finding the receipt or the bill or the paper they needed.

Elizabeth tiptoed into my room, climbed up my ladder, and scrunched into the bottom corner of my bed. I asked her what was wrong.

She asked, "Why are they fighting?"

I said, "They aren't fighting, really. They are just worried about taxes. It happens every year."

"Taxes?" Elizabeth asked.

"Yeah," I explained, sitting up and feeling very wise. "It's money you have to pay the government so we can have wars and schools and bridges, stuff like that."

"No, Justin," Elizabeth said. "Taxes is the kind of car you

take in New York City if you don't have your own car. It's also called a cabbage."

"Well," I said, trying not to laugh at her because of how wise I am, "why would they fight about that?"

"Exactly," Elizabeth said. "Can I have a sleepover here?"

I let her. I even let her sleep on the Pillow of Honor. (Just her head.)

—

April 3, Saturday

Dad's birthday!

Gingy and Poopsie and Elizabeth and I made him a cake while he and Mom worked at the store. Gingy planned a whole dinner of his favorite things so she sent me and Poopsie to the grocery store with a list.

Poopsie is an awesome person to go to the grocery store with. He buys more junk food than any adult I've ever met, even if it is not on the list, and when he can't find something on the list, he hollers its name like it might hear and come running down the aisle and jump in the cart. "Tarragon! Where are you? Mustard seed, give me your hand, Monsieur Mustard Seed!"

He is a total nut. And then he let me get something from

watched the plastic thing to see if a blue line came. One did. So Dr. Carroll said, "Congratulations, Justin! You're pregnant!"

Well, that truly freaked me out. *Pregnant? What the heck? I'm a boy, and also a kid! Pregnant?*

I didn't say anything, because I had too many questions in my head. Mom and Dr. Carroll laughed. Dr. Carroll said, "Just kidding, Justin. You have strep throat."

"Oh," I said.

Mom hugged me and held my hand as we walked out to the car.

It was just that I was out of it, because of being sick, Mom said. She and Dr. Carroll didn't think I really thought I was pregnant.

The thing is, I kind of did.

April 9, Friday

I got to stay home again, even though I felt fine. The rule is if you have a fever one day you get to stay home the next, even if you feel great.

Mom and I watched a movie in the morning and then we had chicken noodle soup for lunch.

Then I got to play video games for a full hour plus.

174

every machine at the exit, even though it cost $2.50 in coins and they were all what Mom calls CLTs (Crummy Little Toys). And he said I didn't even have to share them with Elizabeth. They were all for me.

It wasn't Disney or LEGOLAND. But I don't think I could have had more fun anywhere.

—

April 4, Sunday

Dad's party last night was excellent. He loved everything, all the food and presents and especially the cards made by Elizabeth and me.

Today we had an Easter egg hunt at Montana C.'s house. There were, like, 40 kids there. Luckily she has a huge yard.

Unluckily, she has a trampoline.

Turns out, I no thank you trampolines.

April 5, Monday

Tomorrow is back to school.

Today is buy new shoes and some decent T-shirts without stains all over them for goodness' sake and get a haircut.

I think they do this to kids so we will be relieved to get done with vacation.

—

April 6, Tuesday

Everybody noticed my haircut.

I was wishing for a hat.

But then I started noticing a lot of people had gotten haircuts, so when they said, "Got a haircut, Justin Case?" I said, "Yeah, you too?" And then we could both feel embarrassed.

Not Noah, though. His hair is still extremely large.

For homework we have to write a story about our vacation, but first we have to brainstorm ideas.

My brain stormed and stormed but nothing came to it.

My brain may be the type that takes a while to readjust to school.

I think Ms. Termini does not understand that kind of brain.

It is already three-quarters of the way through the school

year and Ms. Termini still scares the jelly out of me. I guess Mom was wrong about what she said in September, that whole *you'll get used to Ms. Termini soon* thing.

—

April 7, Wednesday

I am not faking.

And it's not just that I am scared to walk Qwerty on my own. I totally am not scared; I just don't enjoy being yanked around. Especially when I feel like my bones are already coming apart at the joints.

Which might be a horrible disease that should be looked at by a doctor, just in case emergency treatment is necessary.

My head hurts, and so does my everything else.

But the worst is swallowing.

I so wish I had Wingnut to cuddle.

—

April 8, Thursday

I stayed home from school. It would've been fun if I didn't feel so lousy.

Mostly I just slept in the morning. Then we went to the doctor's office. She gagged me with a Q-tip. She and Mom and I

All together it added up to more screen time than I usually get in a week.

Sometimes a person needs a day off, Mom said.

She might be the smartest woman in the world.

———

April 10, Saturday

I went to Little League, even though I still have so much more pink medicine to gulp down as fast as possible so I won't have to taste it. Secretly I don't actually hate the taste so horribly much but I am not telling Mom that because she lets me have a gummy worm after each dose to get rid of the disgusting taste.

That's 20 free gummy worms for me.

My friends were happy to see me when I got out of the car at the field. They all yelled, "Justin Case! Justin Case!" and crowded around me until Mom finally said, "Okay, everybody, let go of Justin's face, please."

But then I struck out all four times I was up at bat.

So maybe they got over all that being so happy to see me stuff.

———

April 11, Sunday

We went to the farmers' market. Bartholomew Wiggins and his family were there. Mom said Bartholomew and I could walk around a little ourselves, which made me feel proud to be so grown-up but also a little unhappy because Bartholomew Wiggins is kind of an annoying kid to be stuck with.

And that was even before he offered me free baseball advice.

What I didn't say:

You are the only kid worse than me on our whole team, Bartholomew Wiggins.

What I did say:

Sure, I'd be happy to hear your advice.

What he advised:

Don't swing when you're at bat. You still might strike out, but sometimes you might get walked, and since you're fast, you could even score.

What I said:

Good idea, thanks!

What I thought:

That actually is a good idea.

—

April 12, Monday

I handed in my What I Did on Vacation paper.

Ms. Termini said, "Welcome back, Justin," but it sounded like she was thinking, *I know you were actually not sick on Friday and just stayed home having way too much screen time.*

Then at lunch I heard Montana B. and Montana C. talking about Daisy's birthday party.

Which was yesterday.

Which I did not get invited to.

—

April 13, Tuesday

I couldn't help it.

At recess I blurted out to Daisy, "How was your birthday party?" Her cheeks turned red and she said, "Fine, thank you."

Maybe that was mean of me, but honestly, we really were best friends for a long time and she never didn't invite me to her birthday party before. Today is her actual birthday but we are not in the same class so I didn't even get a cupcake at the end of the day for it.

That made me feel very bad.

And at night, when I thought of it being her birthday, I didn't call her.

And I didn't make her a pop-up card.
Just a plain one. Which I might not
even give her in school tomorrow,
or if I do I might just put it in
her cubby instead of handing
it to her personally.

Too bad if that's nasty. I don't even care.

Sometimes I imagine sending Daisy down to the Way-Back
of the basement and her getting stuck behind The Boiler all by
herself. That's very mean, so I try not to do it except at my
angriest moments.

Like today. Twice.

—

April 14, Wednesday

I am in such big trouble I can't even think.

—

April 15, Thursday

What I did:

Let Qwerty out the back door again

What I was supposed to do:

Take him for a walk

What Qwerty did:

Ran away

What Mom did:

Yelled at me. Then closed her eyes and walked away from me.

What Dad did:

Went all around the neighborhood with me, shouting, "Qwerty! Qwerty!"

What Elizabeth did:

Cried

What I wish I could do:

Turn back the clock

What I do too much:

Lose things

What I miss:

Qwerty

—

April 16, Friday

I was asleep, or maybe I was only half asleep, when I heard Bad Boy outside my window, and then at the front door. I heard his big heavy boots scraping on the front porch, and his long nails scratching the lock of the door. I knew he'd be inside my house in a few seconds, not long enough for me to get to Mom and Dad even though I was on the lower bunk. I was doomed, and I knew it. I scrambled to the corner of my bed, shaking, crying.

Then I heard a growl. Demons? Wolves? I was wide-awake by then. Another growl. My heart was trying to escape my body.

A bark. Then another.

What was going on?

The next thing I heard sounded kind of like a baby crying.

I am, like, the least brave person in the world, but seriously, a baby? How could even a bad guy named Bad Boy hurt a baby? On my front porch?

Without getting my thoughts together or my slippers on, I tumbled out of bed and was down the stairs and opening the front door before the thought hit me that Mom and Dad should be handling this, not me. But it was too late. The door was open only a crack before I got shoved back by a wet, smelly, muddy mess.

Qwerty was back!

I was so happy to see him I forgot to be scared of him, or quiet. I guess I was yelling his name, because Mom and Dad and Elizabeth were suddenly up and in the living room with us, everybody rubbing sleepy eyes and matted dog fur at the same time.

"What happened to you, Qwerty?" Mom asked him, and that's when I noticed: Qwerty had sticks poking out of his face, maybe 30 or 35 of them.

"You look like an hors d'oeuvre, pal," Dad said.

"Looks like he made friends with a porcupine," Mom said.

I started to freak out just a little at that, because, poor Qwerty, and it was all my fault, and what if a porcupine's quills are poisonous to a dog?

"He'll be okay," Mom said. "It will be a long night for us, and especially for him, but he'll be okay. Everything will be okay," she said, and she wrapped her arms around me and held me tight while Dad and Elizabeth did the same thing with Qwerty.

"It's all my fault," I admitted.

"Everybody makes mistakes," Mom whispered back. "I'm sorry I was so hard on you about letting him out."

"No," I said. "You were right to be."

"Well, I don't know about that," she said, and we both wiped our eyes at the same time, which made us smile. "But I do know it takes courage to admit it when you're wrong."

I shrugged, because courage is one thing I know I do not have.

Dad, meanwhile, was working one of the quills out of Qwerty's face. Qwerty sat very still except for quivering a bit, and looked very trustingly into Dad's eyes the whole time. When the quill came free, we all told Qwerty what a good, brave dog he was.

Qwerty looked kind of unsure, but grateful.

There were 34 quills in all. By the end, we were all hugging Qwerty and stroking his filthy fur.

Even me.

April 17, Saturday

Luckily it's the weekend.

We were all exhausted. Especially Qwerty.

But he went to the vet's anyway, for a checkup (he's fine) and a bath (he smells a whole lot better).

I walked him by myself this afternoon. Boy, did I hold that leash tight. And Qwerty hardly yanked me at all.

Maybe we're both growing up.

Or at least getting used to each other.

Mom and Dad talked to a guy about having a fence put up around our yard so sometimes Qwerty can be out there and run around not on his leash.

—

April 18, Sunday

This morning I woke up to stinky breath on my face, and I thought, with my eyes still closed, *Wingnut?*

Then I opened my eyes and saw Qwerty staring at me, wagging his huge windshield-wiper tail — but not jumping up on my bed.

I had slept on the lower bunk not because I was afraid of falling off the top but just in case Qwerty got scared or lonely or had a bad dream about porcupines and needed some company. I actually am being honest.

We stared at each other.

"You kissed a porcupine," I whispered to him.

He kind of whined a little, like he felt foolish about it.

I wasn't sure what to say then, because I didn't want to make him feel stupider about that choice, and I appreciated that he didn't seem to blame me for my part in the fiasco. So instead of saying anything I reached out my hand for him to smell.

He put his cheek down on my palm and rested it there.

Then he ran out of my room because Dad was jangling his leash, ready to go for a run. I stayed in bed and smiled.

—

April 19, Monday

The bad thing about relay races in gym:

People chanting your nickname, "Justin Case," while you run

The good things about relay races in gym:

They are not rope climbing, which is our next unit

Winning (which my team did)

—

April 20, Tuesday

For Earth Day Thursday, we have to write haikus. Haikus are about nature. A haiku that is not about nature is what a senryu is, it turns out, and that is apparently not what we are writing.

Mittens are not "nature," so anybody who wrote a nice haiku about a mitten that got lost actually wrote a senryu and had to start over, even though it was my best poem ever.

This is my stinky haiku:

Dandelions rock

They polka-dot the green grass

For decoration

—

April 21, Wednesday

I know a polka-dot is not nature.

But dandelions are, and so is grass.

And so is *rock*, even though not how I used it.

That's three nature things. But still I got a "see me."
That's what I am going to say to Ms. Termini. I am going to
say, *Yeah, but I used three nature things, and you never said
there can't be anything that's not nature. In the example you
read us, Ms. Termini, there was a "the." "The" is not part of
nature. "The" is . . . Hmm. What the heck is "the"?*

How can I be in third grade and not know what "the" is?

No, I am not going to freak out. I am totally going to stand
up for myself, maybe. I am just going to avoid admitting that I
don't know what "the" is. If possible.

—

April 22, Thursday

She didn't ask me what "the" means. Luckily. But that wasn't even the best news.

The "see me" was because my haiku was chosen.

I wrote the Haiku of the Class.

Which meant I had to read it at the assembly in front of the whole school, along with all the other kids who wrote the Haiku of their Class. Like Daisy. And Elizabeth.

Daisy's haiku:

Hills in the distance

Soaking up the setting sun

Another day ends

Elizabeth's haiku:

Dog poop is stinky

But it is good for the soil

Just watch where you step!

—

April 23, Friday

Elizabeth got the most applause of anybody in the school for her haiku.

186

I was a little jealous but a lot proud.

Especially that my formerly shy little sister would say the word *poop* in front of the whole school.

Mom hung both our haikus on the fridge.

She said she never realized she was raising a couple of poets.

April 24, Saturday

I took Bartholomew Wiggins's advice at Little League.

I just stood there at the plate and didn't move my bat at all.

The first two ups I struck out, but I usually do that anyway, so no big deal. I am used to that long trudge back to the bench.

But on my third time up, an amazing thing happened.

I got a walk!

I didn't trudge back to the bench! I ran to first base!

It was my best-ever day of Little League, even though Carlos popped up and I never made it to second.

All thanks to Bartholomew Wiggins.

What Dad said: "Way to wait for your pitch, Justin!"

What he did: put his arm around my shoulder as we walked to the car after the game.

When we got home the fence around our yard was just about done. We all hung out back there, even Qwerty, and Dad grilled burgers for dinner. It was a great day.

Sometimes life is just perfect.

—

April 25, Sunday

We have relay races again in gym tomorrow.

I should really get some practice.

Right after I finish relaxing and playing these video games.

—

April 26, Monday

I should have practiced.

I hate gym.

I hate Mr. Calabrio.

I hate the word *hustle*.

And I more than anything hate shoelaces that untie and trip a person and make him fall on his butt in front of the whole third grade.

Too bad if *butt* is a bad word.

I think *shoelaces* is a much worse word.

—

April 27, Tuesday

Pajama Day is Friday.

I forgot all about voting for that dumb thing until I had to go miss recess on such a nice day to hang up posters about it.

Maybe I could lie to everybody and say I voted against it, so they will not hate me.

I know lying is wrong but so is making kids come to school in their pajamas.

—

April 28, Wednesday

People seem weirdly excited about Pajama Day.

I don't get it at all.

I'm just glad Xavier Schwartz and Gianni Schicci don't want to beat me up for it.

I don't know about the girls because I am not talking to them. If they don't want to invite me to their parties, that's just fine with me. I don't even care.

—

April 29, Thursday

I know you have to stay silent during a fire drill.

I was totally trying to stay silent.

It was Xavier Schwartz who was talking, saying we should wear glow-in-the-dark pajamas, and did I have some, and I just whispered that yes, I had Batman glow-in-the-darks from last year. I thought that would be the end of it and we could be silent the rest of the time but no, because it turned out that Xavier Schwartz also had glow-in-the-dark Batman pajamas from last year.

What I didn't say: They sold them in the store. Lots of people probably have them.

What I did say: nothing. I just smiled.

But we both got sent to the principal's office, where we had to sit and wait on the bad-kid chairs once again.

I used to be terrified of getting sent to sit on the bad-kid chairs.

At the rate I am going, soon they will name one of the bad-kid chairs after me.

—

April 30, Friday

I wore my glow-in-the-dark Batman pajamas.

So did Xavier Schwartz. (I mean, he wore his. He didn't wear mine, too.)

It was kind of cool, like we were a team or something. We went into the coat closet together when Ms. Termini left the room and we glowed. Then we scrambled back to our seats and nobody told on us, not even my thunderously loud pounding heart.

It was funny seeing everybody in pajamas, to tell the truth. Noah, the lunatic, even wore his big dinosaur slippers. Daisy wore a flannel nightgown. The Montanas wore little shorts with flowers on them and tank tops. Gianni Schicci had grown out of

his glow-in-the-darks so he wore stripey pajamas like a lot of other kids, but his were blue and green on the top and red and orange on the bottoms.

But the funniest was the teachers.

May 1, Saturday

Walked twice and only struck out once.

Out in deep left field, I had my first-ever moment of imagining playing for the Yankees.

But then I got over it.

—

May 2, Sunday

Dad planted begonias and petunias and a bunch of other flowers with silly names this morning. Elizabeth and I helped for a little while but then we got bored so we went inside. The best part of gardening is the bad words Dad says when he is trying to dig out the rocks.

We all had to go out and admire the garden when he was done. It did look good, though too pink in my opinion.

While Dad showered and then napped, I played Atom Blaster. Elizabeth practiced piano. Mom did stuff on her computer.

And Qwerty dug up everything Dad had just planted in the garden.

—

May 3, Monday

There is something worse in gym than relay races.

It is called gymnastics.

There is a reason people don't normally climb up ropes or hang upside down by their knees.

It is called we are not monkeys or bats.

—

May 4, Tuesday

The violin recital is in two weeks.

I am back to thinking about moving to New Jersey.

I have a feeling the orchestra teacher, Mrs. Phillips, would be a big supporter of that idea. Even my best song, which is "How Ya Doin'," is pretty painful for everybody, including me.

I even practiced it.

Once.

Snakey looked ready to attack me. And for the first time ever, all the stuffties were united behind him. Including Bananas.

(Of course, not Wingnut.)

Thinking about how Wingnut would be on my side if I hadn't lost him, I had to put down my violin and be sad for a while. Some people think all there is in life is responsibilities and practicing things, when sometimes a person has to take time to feel bad about his tragedies.

—

May 5, Wednesday

Today is Cinco de Mayo. That is a Mexican holiday.

So we had an assembly and did a dance around a hat.

—

May 6, Thursday

Today is Seis de Mayo.

That is not a holiday anywhere, apparently. So we didn't dance around any clothing at all.

Instead we started writing poems to our mothers, because Sunday is Mother's Day.

We do an awful lot of poetry in third grade. Enough is enough already, I think.

A lot of words that look like they'd rhyme with *mother* don't. Like *bother*. And some words that do rhyme with *mother* are useless, like *brother* and *smother*.

And in student council I voted yes on the bake sale. Because, who would vote against a bake sale?

—

May 7, Friday

My poem for Mom:

> *She is my mother*
>
> *I don't have another*
>
> *Or even a brother*
>
> *Though sometimes she'll smother*
>
> *Me with her kisses and other*
>
> *Mom things, she's my mother!*
>
> *So I love 'er.*

—

May 8, Saturday

I hate my poem.

Maybe if I make her a pop-up card to go with it, she'll get distracted and not notice the poem.

The last line doesn't rhyme. Ms. Termini called it a slant rhyme. She said I was using a poetic license. But I never got a poetic license so there's no way I can use mine. Anyway, what the heck is a "slant rhyme"?

I have a feeling the "slant" in that sentence of "You used a slant rhyme" is teacher-talk for "bad . . ." or, "Tough tomatoes on you, pal, that doesn't . . ."

Maybe I will quickly make Mom some jewelry or clothes or some food with wheat germ in it like she likes. And I could just slip my dumb slanted poem under her door tonight when she isn't looking, and maybe she won't find it for a while.

Yes, that is definitely what I am going to do, and then I will have done my weekend homework by giving her the card without having to face her about the slantiness of my poem.

If Elizabeth's poem is better than mine, I will be so ashamed.

May 9, Sunday

It isn't stealing if you pay.

That's what I told Elizabeth, but she isn't sure. I am not 100% sure, either, but I am, like, 87–89% sure we didn't steal those flowers from Mrs. Edmundson's yard. Because we left her $3.47 in pennies from our combined penny collections right where the flowers used to be.

How else were two kids who can't drive and don't have permission to walk into town supposed to get flowers for their mother on Mother's Day? (I gave 174 pennies, because I am older so I wanted to give extra.)

I wanted to also give Mom something that would last, so I took the bear down from my shelf, the one I painted at Noah's party that is my best work of art ever. I love it more than any of my other paint-on-pottery. I wrapped it up in wrapping paper. It is not a cube or a box; it is bear-shape, so the wrapping job was extremely difficult and took a very lot of tape.

I will miss having that bear on my own shelf but as much as I love that thing, I love my mom infinity times more.

So it is worth it.

I think.

May 10, Monday

She loved it.

All the presents.

She even climbed up to the top bunk and cuddled me and said she loved finding the beautiful poem on her floor when she woke up, and she will treasure the bear forever and the flowers as long as they last. She put them in her best vase.

Then she read to me. That is maybe a baby thing because for goodness' sake I have known how to read myself for years now, but I still loved it anyway. It was very cozy.

So yesterday was a very good Mother's Day for me, too.

Especially because Elizabeth didn't even write a poem. She made a trivet out of mosaic tiles. It was extremely lumpy but I just complimented the color pattern instead of mentioning how much pots would wobble on it. She looked very proud when I told her it was a good pattern.

Now I am lying here, not sleeping, but for once not because I am scared. I've got Snakey on the lookout and Qwerty down below. No, I am not sleeping because of smiling.

—

May 11, Tuesday

The answer to the violin musical question of "How Ya Doin' " is:

Not well.

Very not well at all.

—

May 12, Wednesday

Gianni Schicci and Xavier Schwartz are BOTH coming over for

a playdate tomorrow.

It is a favor to their moms, who have to do some PTA thing at school.

I am not overreacting. My mother does not know those guys.

I have to pray for an earthquake or something.

I told Qwerty about it while I was walking him.

The good thing about a dog:

How much he agrees, automatically, with whatever you are saying.

The bad thing about a mom:

How much she doesn't.

—

May 13, Thursday

I knew it.

Didn't I tell her it would be a disaster?

And I am not even talking about the window that broke from practicing forward rolls on my bed and Gianni's foot going through it (the window, not the bed). A window can be replaced, good as new, no problem, is what Mom said.

What I am talking about is the damage to Snakey.

—

May 14, Friday

This morning at the cubbies, Gianni Schicci and his mom were waiting. Snakey was in a big blue bag. His eye had been sewn back on and the rip in his neck had gotten stitches. Gianni had sworn that his mom was an ace at sewing up stuffties because she is a doctor who works in the emergency room at the hospital so she gets a lot of practice on people.

I tried to act like it was no big deal again, so Gianni and now his mom wouldn't know I still love my stuffties, even the ferocious ones who barely cry when they get their eye popped off and their neck ripped open while being used as a sword even though I said, "Please stop using my snake as a sword" in my most serious *I mean it, mister* voice.

Gianni's mom whispered something to Gianni. He fished around in the blue bag and pulled out a small wrapped thing. I wasn't sure what to do about that because it wasn't my birthday; it wouldn't even be my birthday for another month and no way was Gianni Schicci getting invited to it, not after what he did to Snakey. Probably not even before that, but definitely not after. So why was he handing me a present?

He didn't look too happy about it, either.

His mom said, "Gianni is very sorry he was rough with your stuffed animal, aren't you, Gianni?"

"Sorry," Gianni said.

I wanted to say that's okay but since it was a lie, it got stuck.

"Gianni of all people knows how precious a person's stuffed animals are, right, Gianni?"

Gianni just turned funny colors at that.

"So we repaired your snake as best we could," she continued, "but we also went to Big Top and Gianni bought you a stuffed chipmunk. With his own money. He has been saving up to buy the stuffed chipmunk for himself, but he would like to give it to you as an apology. Right, Gianni?"

Gianni opened his mouth to say "yes" or maybe "right" but it was a lie so it got stuck.

Instead he shoved the package toward me.

I took it gently. "You don't have to . . ." I started to explain.

"It's okay," Gianni said sadly, and walked into class.

I put Snakey and the still-wrapped chipmunk into my cubby and followed him in.

—

May 15, Saturday

On our way to the outfield, I called Gianni's name.

He rolled his eyes and waited for me.

"We can share it," I said. "The chipmunk."

"Whatever," he said.

"Or it could be yours, and I would just keep it for you, for a while."

"I don't really care that much about stuffties anymore."

I nodded. I was about to say, *Yeah, me neither*, but accidentally I said, "I do."

"Yeah, well, but only really good ones," he said.

"Yeah," I agreed. "You had to use your own money?"

"I'm working on self-control," he said.

"Oh," I said. "I'm working on being brave."

We nodded at each other.

Then we had to turn around and pay attention to the game.

I struck out twice and walked once, but because of the walk I got to third base, my best game ever.

May 16, Sunday

Mom and Dad are going away. They are all packed already and they signed the permission slip for my class trip to the science museum, and they have tickets for the plane and everything. They swear they told us about this many, many

times but them going away for a full week is not something I
would just forget. What kind of parents go away for a week and
leave their children all alone?

Okay, fine, I get it that Gingy and Poopsie are staying with
us, so technically we are not being left all alone. But Gingy and
Poopsie are not parents. They are Grands. It is a whole different
thing.

Elizabeth is totally psyched.

I am not so sure.

I am picturing a week of goofiness, no bedtimes, and food
that jiggles. It could be great but it could be chaos.

Or it could be both.

I didn't even know I was going on a class trip to the science
museum, though that did sound slightly familiar.

I am not getting all my memos, Mom said might be the
problem.

—

May 17, Monday

While Mom and Dad were on a plane flying away from me, I
learned a terrible thing. We have to climb up the rope. All the
way up to the piece of white tape wrapped around it way up
high, a dangerously far distance from the gym floor. Or we don't

graduate from third grade.

I do not think it is good to encourage kids to be that far from the ground. Seriously. Have they thought this whole activity through?

I think it would be good if my parents call us from Bermuda where they are having their first-ever vacation together since I was born and say Bermuda is beautiful and they miss us so Gingy and Poopsie are bringing us down there to our new house.

Poopsie says nobody wears pants in Bermuda. I am pretty sure he is making that up. They walk around in their underwear? Gingy, who usually tells Poopsie to stop riling up the children with his nonsense, said it was true and Bermuda is famous for nobody wearing pants. Seriously? Even the visitors? I don't know if Mom and Dad were aware of this Bermuda fact before planning their trip. Probably my grandparents are just being weird.

But even if not, walking around in underwear might be better than climbing a rope all the way up higher than Mr. Calabrio's bald head.

Or going to Gianni's laser-tag birthday party Sunday.

Even the invitation to it looks too wild for me.

I don't want to say no to him without a good reason or he will think I don't appreciate his gift of the chipmunk, which I do. I named him Schicci and let him sleep on the Pillow of Honor last night. (The chipmunk, not Gianni.)

But I do have a great idea of what to buy Gianni as a gift.

—

May 18, Tuesday

If I had to choose which is worst of:

A) Climbing a rope up higher than a gym teacher's bald head

B) Practicing my squeaky violin

C) Hanging upside down by my knees so my shirt falls up

D) Getting driven somewhere by Gingy, the slowest driver on the planet

E) Walking my drooly dog every day because my parents went away

I would have to choose

F) All of the above

Welcome to my life as a third grader.

—

May 19, Wednesday

I fell off.

Xavier Schwartz was trying to teach me to hang by my knees on the jungle gym in the playground at lunch. He said it was all a matter of squeezing your feet toward your butt. Well, apparently I didn't squeeze hard enough because just when I had the thought of *I'm doing it!* I was flying headfirst onto the black playground mat.

Everybody was standing above me asking if I was okay but I truthfully didn't know. My teeth all hurt and the kids were making me seasick by swaying, so I had to close my eyes.

I realized I was walking into school with my arms around shoulders. Then I realized the shoulders belonged to Noah and Daisy, and also that my legs had been replaced with overcooked strands of fettuccine. I figured out that I was obviously dreaming, because I was barely friends with Daisy anymore and also legs don't just become pasta. So I closed my eyes.

When I opened them I was in the nurse's office, lying on a cot. What was making me feel sick was the nurse's clock. Instead of going *tick-tock-tick-tock* on a steady beat, it would go *tick* and then wait a while in silence. Then in a rush it would suddenly tap out *tocktocktocktocktock-tick-tock-tick* . . . and then go silent for a while longer.

That's why I threw up.

I tried to explain that to the nurse but she didn't understand. That's why she pulled out my emergency contact card and I got picked up from the nurse's office by Gingy and Poopsie.

—

May 20, Thursday

I have to go to the science museum trip.

It is, like, the biggest trip of the whole school year.

Gingy called Mom and Dad in Bermuda to let me talk to them about it. I told them I have a little headache. That's all. I can't miss the trip. I forgot to ask them about the pants issue, because of thinking about this trip.

We are supposed to bring five dollars and we can go to the gift shop. Noah says it is the coolest gift shop ever.

And I promised I would sit with him on the bus.

I have to convince Gingy to let me go.

I CANNOT miss this trip today.

—

May 21, Friday

I should have missed that trip.

The bus ride to the science museum was terrible. My skull was squishing down on my brain the whole time. Then we had to pull over on the side of the road while a kid threw up onto the side-of-the-highway grass.

The kid was me.

I rested my face against the cool window for the rest of the trip, and Noah got to be seat buddies with somebody else because I had to be up in the front row.

Then at the museum there was a tour, and the tour leader's voice was very squealy. It made me feel like my eyes were different sizes from each other. I had to sit down for a few minutes to stop the floor from bobbling.

By the time I stood up my group was gone.

I tried to follow them, but that museum has a lot of doorways and choices of which way to go. I saw some interesting stuff like chairs stacked up higher than my head and a vending machine that had nothing in it but empty metal spirals. Also some exhibits. But nobody from my school.

So finally I sat down near some rocks from the moon.

That's where Ms. Burns found me.

Everybody else was already on the bus, and there I was, next to pieces of moon.

And then we had another long pukey bus trip ahead of us.

Gingy should not take advice from a third grader. I don't know what is wrong with that grandmother.

—

May 22, Saturday

I stayed home from Little League. Apparently I have something called a concussion. That is a brain bruise.

All my stuffties stayed quiet and stared at me. I think they were very worried. None of them had ever heard of a brain bruise before.

Gingy made me Jell-O.

I accidentally admitted to her that I actually do not enjoy food that jiggles. She was very surprised and then very amused. She said she has a horror of jiggly food, too. She'd be happy never to make Jell-O again. She only did it because she thought I loved it. She said, "Why didn't you ever tell me? We could've avoided so much unpleasant jiggling!"

She sent Poopsie and Elizabeth out to buy ice cream, instead. They came home with four quarts plus six containers of toppings.

We tried to gobble it all up before Mom and Dad get home tonight. Poopsie said that is known as eating the evidence.

It was not possible to eat all that evidence.

But I don't think Mom and Dad will be mad anyway.

—

May 23, Sunday

Mom and Dad brought us T-shirts and key chains from Bermuda. It's not that I missed them so much, it's just that I was really happy to have them home. That's why I let them do all that cuddling. They missed us a lot.

They said nobody wanders around in just underpants. Poopsie tried to explain his way out of what he told us, but Elizabeth and I know the truth. When I grow up, I want to be a grandfather like him, full of nonsense and laughing.

Mom wasn't sure Gianni would like the present I picked out, but I was. I think she was worried my brain bruise was dementing me a little.

The laser tag would have made me dizzy even with a totally

unbruised brain. The party was in a huge dark place with big, hanging, heavy bags that kept wapping into us and it was all the boys in third grade.

On the way home, as I sorted through my loot bag in the backseat, I told Mom it was kind of fun especially getting picked first, but that my heart almost crashed out from being scared of getting killed with a laser.

She said, "You wouldn't actually get killed, Justin."

I said, "I know. Not actually killed. Just pretend. I was pretending."

She smiled all loving at me and said I have a great imagination.

I told her, "Yeah, well, my heart would sometimes love a break from being stuck inside somebody with such a great imagination."

"I bet," she said.

—

May 24, Monday

I think the reason Gianni picked me first for his laser-tag team yesterday even though I had never played laser tag before is not what he said, that I am the fastest boy. Xavier Schwartz is just about as fast, really, and he's also Gianni's best friend. I think he chose me first because when I handed him his present, he recognized the size and shape of the box and realized I'd gotten him what he had been wishing for but not telling anybody he wanted for his birthday.

This is how I know that:

We bumped into each other hiding behind a bag about halfway through the party. We were holding our lasers up and both of us had sweaty heads. Catching his breath, he said, "Did you give me what I gave you?"

"Yeah," I said.

"What'd you name yours?"

I so wished in that second I had named him Chip, like I had been planning to. I almost lied. But lying makes my stomach hurt and if I threw up in front of everybody one more time this week, I would probably never get invited to a birthday party again in my life. So I shrugged and mumbled, "Schicci."

Gianni smiled his huge smile that made his dimples sink in. "I'll name mine Case," he said.

—

May 25, Tuesday

The second-worst thing about the recital:

The sweat ball that dripped off my nose onto my violin

The second-best thing about the recital:

Gingy and Poopsie gave me a king-size pack of Twizzlers, after

The worst thing about the recital:

Playing "How Ya Doin' " with very few of the actual notes

The best thing about the recital:

Fishing Montana C.'s retainer out of her cello before the concert

Tied with:

The nice thing Montana C. said about me after I held up that huge cello over my head and caught the retainer with my hair, right above my bruised brain:

You're my hero,

Justin Case!

May 26, Wednesday

Xavier Schwartz said that he is going to get me.

He said that I am a Girlfriend Stealer.

I have no idea what it means that he is going to get me, or why I am a girlfriend stealer, but I know neither one is good news.

Less than a month until the end of school. If I don't climb up the rope to the white tape line, which I can't anyway, I won't be in Xavier Schwartz's class next year.

That is the only bright side I can see in the world right now.

—

May 27, Thursday

He thinks I stole Montana C.

That's what Gianni told me.

How could I steal a whole Montana C.?

—

May 28, Friday

At lunch Xavier and Gianni walked over to me and Noah. I thought for sure they were going to beat us up.

So before they got a chance, I said, "Before you beat me up, there is something I have to say."

"Okay," Xavier said. They waited. Noah waited. I waited, too.

"What I have to say is this," I said, wishing for my bruised brain to please come up with something.

"Is what?" Xavier Schwartz asked.

"Is," I said. "There is no such thing as boyfriends or

girlfriends in third grade. There is only friends. You can have girl-space-friends but not girlfriends. So I can't be a Girlfriend Stealer, because there's no girlfriend to steal."

All three of them stared at me.

"Like from another planet?" Gianni asked.

So we all stared at him.

"You said, 'girl space-friends,' " Gianni explained.

"Yeah," Xavier said, shoving him. "If you meet a girl martian, you can ask her out."

"What?" Gianni asked. "Justin Case said . . ."

And while they argued, Noah and I slipped away, and then the bell rang for the end of recess.

Luckily it is a long weekend so we don't run the risk of getting clobbered for three full days.

—

May 29, Saturday

We're going to Gingy and Poopsie's beach condo.

No worries about Jell-O this time.

Just sharks.

Also, snoring.

—

May 30, Sunday

No sign of sharks so far.

I think the snoring is scaring them off.

(Looking on the bright side.)

May 31, Monday

Elizabeth has a new loose tooth.

I learned to dive for coins.

Poopsie learned to not cannonball into the pool, because even though it makes Elizabeth and me laugh, it annoys the grown-ups.

June 1, Tuesday

The thing I hate even worse than getting beaten up by Xavier Schwartz and Gianni Schicci is wondering if they actually will beat me up, and how bad it will feel if they do, and trying to figure out what to do just in case they come toward me with *we are going to beat you up* looks on their faces.

Of course, I haven't gotten beaten up yet so maybe that will turn out to be even worse than worrying about it.

Maybe we will get lost on the way to school this morning and end up in Guatemala, which is in Central America, which is very, very far away.

—

June 2, Wednesday

The Good News:

1. Xavier Schwartz and Gianni Schicci apparently forgot about beating me up

2. I let lots of people cut in the rope line in gym, which had two good results:

a) People seemed to like me for that

b) I didn't get a turn to try climbing the rope

3. I am apparently good at outlining, which is what we are learning, so

a) I got a Superstar

b) I got a check plus

c) I got to go relax in the library corner instead of reviewing outlining

The Bad News:

1. Even Bartholomew Wiggins climbed up to the white

line on the rope

    a) He was my best hope

for another kid failing

    b) I was rooting against

him. That is a lot like

a), I know, but if you put a),

you have to put a

b). Trust me,

I am an

outlining

Superstar. Just

not a rope-

climbing

Superstar

    2. There's always tomorrow for all the bad things that didn't happen today

—

June 3, Thursday

Elizabeth's tooth seems to have tightened up. I told her not to worry, sometimes that happens, but eventually it reloosens and then it will fall out with less problems than when it goes straight loose-looser-loosest out.

She smiled and said, "Thanks, Justin. Phew!" like I was so wise.

I was actually just making that up. I have no idea if it's true.

———

June 4, Friday

At recess, Xavier Schwartz came over to where I was wedging twigs into the fence and asked, "You know why I hated you, right?"

"Because you think I am a Girlfriend Stealer or something, but I — "

"No," Xavier interrupted. "Because I like Montana C. — well, I mean, everybody likes Montana C., but I have liked her *liked her* since kindergarten — and now Montana C. likes you."

My whole body started sweating in one big burst.

"Okay," I said.

"Okay," he agreed.

"Do you still hate me?"

Xavier thought about it for a few seconds. "Nah," he said. "I've moved on."

"Phew," I said.

Then we went down to the lower playground together and joined the new game: Perilous Penguins from Pluto. Everybody played, including Gianni and Montana C. and the other girls and even Noah, because he loves penguins even more than he hates runny-aroundy games.

Gianni said I didn't tag him when I absolutely did, but I was just like, okay. Because, considering everything, I felt really overflowingly good.

June 5, Saturday

We have to plan my birthday party, for two weeks from now, when I might be a third-grade graduate plus one day, or else a third-grade repeater who just likes to keep his feet on the floor where they belong, thank you very much.

The Three Big Questions Are:

1. What will be the theme/activity?
2. Who should be invited?
3. Will some of those from (2) be girls?

The Three Big Answers So Far Are:

1. I don't know.
2. I don't know.

3. I don't know.

4. I don't know.

I know there is no fourth question, but if there were, I'm sure I would not know the answer to that one, either.

—

June 6, Sunday

Elizabeth had a nightmare last night. She came climbing up my ladder. To wake me up, she placed her hand on my cheek. I jolted up.

"I think a bad guy is in the house," she whispered.

"Bad Boy?" I asked, my heart starting to pound against my ribs.

"Who?" she asked.

I took a deep, calming breath like Mom always says to do, in for five, out for five. "Why do you think there's a bad guy?"

"I heard him," she whispered.

"Where?" I asked. "In the Way-Back of the basement? Near The Boiler?"

Elizabeth's eyes opened wide. "I don't know," she said.

"Well," I said to her as patiently as I could, "what exactly did you hear?"

"Kind of a splurching sound," she whispered with her hand

over her mouth.

"Oh," I said, relieved. Bad Boy does not make any splurching sounds. He is more of a clomper. I realized right away Elizabeth had just had a nightmare. "I think I know what it is."

"What?" she asked.

"I think it is a bad guy named Splurch," I told her. For a second I thought maybe I made a bad choice, because her face turned whitish-bluish, and her eyes reddened. That was a bad combination of colors for Elizabeth. But I had a plan, and for some reason I was pretty sure it was going to work. "The good news," I told her, "is that I know how to defeat Splurch."

"You do?" she whispered. "How?"

"You have to call Mr. Magoolicuddy."

"Who?"

I was totally making this up as I went along but I nodded like it was as easy as $3 \times 8 = 24$. "You just say three times fast, 'Mr. Magoolicuddy! Mr. Magoolicuddy! Mr. Magoolicuddy!' and he comes, and he'll get rid of Splurch."

"Really?" She didn't look at all convinced.

"Absolutely," I said, as confident as I could. "Try it."

"Okay," she said. "Mr. Magoolicuddy! Mr. Magoolicuddy! Mr. Magoolicuddy!"

Then we sat still in my bed, listening to the silence.

"Justin," she said. "I think Mr. Magoolicuddy is imaginary."

"Of course Mr. Magoolicuddy is imaginary," I told her. "He has to be. Splurch is imaginary. If Mr. Magoolicuddy weren't imaginary, how would he fight and defeat an imaginary bad guy?"

I watched Elizabeth consider this for a minute. Slowly she lowered her hands from her face and said, "Good point."

Then she smiled.

And she curled up like a little question mark at the foot of my bed and went right to sleep.

Today, twice she said to me, "Mr. Magoolicuddy," and we both cracked up but we wouldn't tell Mom and Dad the secret.

—

June 7, Monday

Mom says I have to finalize my birthday party list and theme.

It is hard to finalize something you haven't started.

Maybe my theme could be: There are no ropes you have to climb, no bad guys in the world, and The Boiler was removed from the Way-Back of our basement.

Maybe they don't make paper plates and napkins to match that exact theme, but at least we wouldn't have to have a piñata massacre.

—

June 8, Tuesday

I tried.

I really did try. I don't care what Mr. Calabrio says. Or how squinched Ms. Termini's eyebrows are at me. Or what the other kids think. I tried to get up that rope. I honestly don't want to be a third-grade failure.

I held my hands one on top of the other like Mr. Calabrio said to (a billion times). When I tried to get up one foot at a time, the rope kept swaying away and almost dumped me right on my butt on the gym floor. But I held on tight. I heard Montana C. yell, "Just jump!" So I just jumped.

Both feet caught the rope and for a minute, okay, maybe a second, I was swinging across the gym on that rope.

And then my hands gave up.

If I could control the rope, make it just hold still, maybe I could do it. But when there is no earth beneath my feet and I am loose and swinging across in the world, I panic. I can't help it. I just feel like, *Get me down! I'm not safe! Help!* The last thing I could possibly do is pull myself up higher.

I feel too loose and swinging across the world in general. Why would I add to the problem on purpose? That is what I don't get and never will.

—

June 9, Wednesday

I decided, while I was walking Qwerty, to just go ahead and invite everybody I like to my birthday party. Boys, girls, I don't care. After the gym humiliation probably none of them will want to come to my party anyway, so it really doesn't matter.

The theme I chose is a farm theme.

I am not actually interested in farms but there was such a cool-looking rooster piñata in the catalog Mom showed me to choose from, I just went ahead and chose a farm theme. Mom ordered the stuff on the internet. She asked, "You sure?" right before she pressed SEND and that was when I remembered I didn't even want a piñata.

But I said, "Yes, I am sure. I have been really wanting a farm theme."

I don't even know what activities you can have at a farm-theme party but it would have been too weird to suddenly be like, *No, but can I just have the rooster piñata to keep?*

On the other hand, since probably nobody will want to come to my party, I will be able to keep the rooster piñata all for myself.

Also the stack of paper plates with cows on them.

—

June 10, Thursday

I woke up feeling like I was falling off the rope. I knew it right then, before I even opened my eyes: I am never going to be brave enough to climb up that darn rope. I could feel the rough bits biting into my palms, and then as much as I tried to think about being safe in my bed for another hour still, my body imagined that rope swinging across the whole gym, with me dangling off it and everybody watching me not get up it until I fell off it.

I really needed Wingnut right then, so much, because all the other stuffties were just staying silent. Snakey was refusing to even look at me, his glassy eyes turned away. The Pillow of Honor sat empty beside me. Bananas tilted her head sympathetically, so I picked her up. She was the President of the Bed, I figured. Maybe she'd have some wisdom in that stuffed monkey brain of hers.

"I'm scared," I whispered.

She looked at me like, *Yeah, everybody knows that about you.*

"I have to climb the rope," I whispered. "Tomorrow is my last chance."

So, Bananas was clearly thinking, *climb it.*

"Easy for you to think," I said. "You're a monkey. I'm not. And the other thing I am not is brave."

Bananas shrugged. Like, *So what?* Like, *Climb it anyway.*

"Yeah, thanks for the advice," I said, and tossed her down toward the foot of my bed. She landed upside down half over

228

Snakey and half on Schicci.

I don't know why I expected to get real help for a real rope and a real problem from somebody made of felt and stuffing and pretending, anyway.

—

June 11, Friday

"Only one kid still has to climb up the rope," Mr. Calabrio announced, staring down at his clipboard. "Let's all cheer for Justin!"

Oh, great. Awesome. Just what I needed.

"Justin Case! Justin Case!" some kids were cheering. Mostly the runny-aroundy boys. "Justin Case!"

I clutched the rope with my two hands.

"You can do it, Justin!" I heard somebody say. I opened my eyes, which made me realize they'd been closed. Right in front of me, across the mat, Daisy smiled. "You can," she said again.

If my heart manages to break through my ribs and land on the mat between me and Daisy, I thought, *I would probably be excused from rope climbing.*

"Up you go," Mr. Calabrio bellowed.

I'm scared, said my own voice inside my head.

That's okay, answered Bananas's voice. *Climb up anyway.*

I closed my eyes, clutched the rope, and bent my knees. The rope swung away but I grabbed it with my legs.

"Climb," some kids yelled, while others kept going with "Justin Case! Justin Case!"

I let go with my left hand and, quick as I could, grabbed on above my right. Then I crunched my knees closer to my belly and wiggled up a little.

I can't.

I waited to hear Bananas's voice answer. Nothing. My fingers were starting to lose their grip.

I can't, I thought again. *I'm not brave enough.*

Just as I was about to let go of the rope and fall down on the gym floor, I heard a different voice inside my head.

It was Wingnut's, and it said, *Pretend.*

Pretend what? I asked the voice, while at the same time thinking this was a very bad moment to be having an imaginary conversation with a lost stuffed dog.

Pretend you're brave.

I'm too scared, I answered, sliding down a little.

If you weren't scared, Wingnut's voice answered mine, *you wouldn't need to be brave.*

I couldn't argue with that. So I decided to do what Wingnut

suggested.

I'm brave, I pretended. I'm as brave as Xavier Schwartz. I wiggled up a little. *I'm as brave as Gianni Schicci.* I wiggled up a little more. *I am way braver than Noah, and Bartholomew Wiggins. I am braver than cute little Montana B. and Willow, braver than Carlos (as well as more freckly), braver than stuffy-nosed Penelope Ann Murphy. I am braver than Daisy, way braver. She is nowhere near as brave as I am. I am braver than Montana C.! Well, maybe not braver, but almost as brave . . .*

And then I realized people were cheering. I gripped the rope hard and that's when I felt it: something smooth wrapped around the rough rope. I opened my eyes and stared at the piece of white tape — under my fingers.

I did it!

I really did it!

I climbed the rope!

I looked down at everybody, all my cheering friends, and saw the tops of their heads. Way down under my sneakers.

It turns out climbing down is not part of the test. Jumping off, or maybe it was falling, is okay, too. Better than okay, actually. Great.

June 12, Saturday

All day I kept thinking, *I did it.*

A couple of times I thought, *I'm hungry* or, *I wish I could have unlimited screen time* or, *I wonder how fish clean themselves*, but then I went right back to *I did it!*

—

June 13, Sunday

Elizabeth lost her tooth but kept it (in her hand) this time. It didn't hurt, she explained to Mom and Dad, because it had tightened up and then reloosened, which gives you a pain-free tooth-losing experience. They started to argue but she held up her hand and said, "Justin explained the whole thing to me already."

She looked pretty cute sitting there so serious, with that big space in the front of her mouth. Then she said, "Well, I guess I accomplished my kindergarten goal."

Mom asked, "Oh? What was your kindergarten goal, sweetheart?"

"Improve my scissor skills and lose some teeth," she said. "And I sure did both!"

"You sure did," Dad said, then turned to me. "Did you

have a third-grade goal, Justin?"

"I don't know," I said.

"You can think about it," Elizabeth suggested, "and get back to us."

—

June 14, The Last Monday of Third Grade

We had to sign up for what to bring in for our class party on Friday, the last day of school. I signed up for gummy bears. The gummy bears from our store are the best; everybody says so. I sign up for that every year.

This is going to be a big week of parties: Wednesday, my in-school birthday celebration. Thursday, student council party. Friday, last day of school party. And Saturday, my actual birthday party.

It turns out everybody is coming.

Well, everybody except Penelope Ann Murphy, who has to go to her aunt's wedding. Which is fine. If I had to get one no, she would be my first choice.

Kind of funny when I remember how I used to feel about Xavier Schwartz and Gianni Schicci.

—

June 15, The Last Tuesday of Third Grade

We were playing Perilous Penguins from Pluto at recess. Xavier and Montana C. and I were all hiding in the shade of the big willow tree on the upper playground.

"Nobody can catch us," Montana C. whispered.

"We rock," Xavier whispered.

"Yeah," I whispered.

Then we ran out and chased everybody until we got to the next level, which was Muckraking Monkeys from Mars.

June 16, The Last Wednesday of Third Grade

My mom came with cupcakes, even though my birthday is not until Saturday. Last year I didn't get a party in school and apparently Mom could tell I was disappointed about that. She said I wasn't very "subtle" about my feelings about it, which means *please stop talking about that, Justin, you are driving me nuts.*

So this year she came in and gave out the cupcakes while I sat on the stool in the front of the classroom. Everybody sang "Happy Birthday" and didn't take a bite until I made my wish, blew out the candle, and bit mine first. Then, with frosting on their faces (except Montana B., who is a very neat eater), they raised their hands to tell me why they were happy I was born.

Gianni is happy I was born because I am smart so when he didn't know an answer, he copied what I had written down. Ms. Termini dropped her mouth open at that. Montana B. thinks I am funny and sweet. Penelope Ann thinks I am kind and she is also happy I made it up the rope; she had all her fingers crossed for me. Montana C. said I am fun and a fast runner. Xavier Schwartz said, "I am happy Justin Case was born because he is my friend."

———

June 17, The Last Thursday of Third Grade

We got certificates.

Also, pizza.

Turns out it was kind of a good thing to be a good class representative.

Especially because I didn't mess up in any major way, as far as I know.

And also because there were ice-cream sandwiches.

June 18, The Last Friday/Last Anything Day of Third Grade

I woke up because of the booming. I thought maybe our house had exploded. It was dark in my room so I had to feel around with my hands while my eyes adjusted to being open, in the dark, in the middle of the night. The ceiling hadn't collapsed on me, apparently. All my stuffties were where they were supposed to be (well, except of course Wingnut) and everything was still and quiet.

Must've been a bad dream, I told myself when a flash of light lit up my room (especially Snakey's glassy uneven eyes), and two seconds later, *Ka-Blaragh!* went the thunder.

Just a storm, I explained to myself. *Nothing to worry about.*

And those noises downstairs? Those are probably just part of the storm, too. Even though they are in the kitchen. And they sound like somebody slamming stuff around in there. *I don't need to worry*, I told myself.

I was sitting bolt upright in my bed by then, chewing on my blanket.

Qwerty will scare away any bad guys, I reminded myself. *That is the whole point of Qwerty. Or at least the whole original point.*

Flash of light, another booming crack of thunder, then more stuff being banged in the kitchen.

Or maybe it was a clomping sound.

Bad Boy!

And then I heard the scariest sound of all. It was Qwerty, whimpering like when he got porcupined.

All my stuffties looked terrified. Even Snakey. Especially when I edged toward the ladder.

I explained that I had to go see what was happening to Qwerty. I promised to be careful. But I had to go.

Snakey smiled at me, showing his venomous stuffed teeth. He understood.

I crept down the stairs, skipping the third one because it squeaks. I flattened myself against the wall between the living room and the kitchen, took a deep breath, and peeked around the corner. There was garbage thrown all around the kitchen.

238

The garbage can was on its side and the white liner had been ripped apart.

I whipped my head out of there and noticed that one of Mom's Valentine pillows from the couch had been destroyed — all the stuffing was spread around the living room and the velvet outside was scattered in strips.

But no sign of Bad Boy. Or Qwerty.

I strained my ears, listening. It was hard to hear anything over the pounding of my heart but eventually I heard one little whimper. It was coming from downstairs.

In the basement.

Oh, great.

I tiptoed slowly down the stairs. If Bad Boy wanted to mess up our house, throw our garbage around, and ruin one of Mom's favorite new red velvet pillows, okay.

But he was not allowed to torture my dog.

On my way down the stairs there was another lightning/thunder explosion. That did not help my nerves one bit. In fact, I had to stop and sit down on the steps. *Just give me a second to collect myself* popped into my head, and as I was trying to remember where I had heard that phrase, I was interrupted by more whimpering from the basement.

Okay, okay, I thought. And step-by-step went closer to it.

I didn't want to turn on the basement light because that would wreck my surprise attack on Bad Boy. But I did grab the flashlight from where it was plugged in right near the washing machine. I turned it on and pointed it at the basement floor.

And then I stopped. To listen, I told myself. But I knew it was also to try to gather some courage.

I heard some breathing. I couldn't tell if it was human breathing or dog breathing, but I knew where it was coming from.

Behind The Boiler.

"Qwerty," I whispered. Dogs have better hearing than people. I had to gamble that Qwerty would hear me before Bad Boy.

He whimpered but didn't budge.

I took a step closer. Then another. Then another.

Qwerty was whimpering louder and louder, and then his huge tail started thumping as he peeked out and saw me. I knew if Bad Boy was back there with him, about to dump him in The Boiler to Boil him, this tail thumping would alert him and I'd get Boiled, too. I had to decide quick whether to run back upstairs to safety.

Before I could think, my hand raised the flashlight to shine it in Bad Boy's eyes.

He wasn't there.

I shined it all around, behind that grumbling Boiler, over by the shelves, back toward the washer and dryer. No sign of Bad Boy.

"Come out, you coward!" I yelled to him. "What are you scared of? Me?"

Qwerty crawled toward me on his belly, crying, and rested his head on my bare foot.

"Well, I'm not scared of you, Bad Boy!" I yelled. "You leave us alone!"

Still nothing, no response. "Some bad guy you are!" I yelled. "Scared of a kid in pajamas with a flashlight? Scared of the most worried kid in the whole third grade?"

He was gone.

My flashlight flashed across a dark little lump behind The Boiler. I pointed the flashlight right at the lumpy little thing. It wasn't moving. Neither was I. I made myself take a step closer to get a better look, but I couldn't tell what it was. The fire in the bottom of The Boiler flashed threateningly. I squinched my eyes closed and, trying not to shake too much, reached carefully behind The Boiler. My heart was pounding so hard as my fingers touched something slightly squishy and damp. I took a deep breath and grabbed it.

It was Wingnut.

Qwerty whimpered and nudged me with his nose but I was busy.

"Wingnut!" I whispered. He had dirt smudged all over him and his front left paw was chewed away and his nose was hanging by a thread. Also, he smelled terrible.

I hugged him close anyway, right up to my face. "You look a mess, Wingnut," I whispered to him. "But I have never been so happy to see somebody in my whole life."

I sat down on the floor holding Wingnut and petting Qwerty, who was shaking all over. "What are you scared of, you silly dog, huh?" I asked him. "Bad Boy?"

Then the thunder rumbled again and that huge dog jumped into my lap, almost knocking me over, his whole body shivering.

"The thunder?" I asked.

He whimpered.

I held him close and explained the rain cycle to him until he calmed down.

Then we went upstairs and the three of us — me, Wingnut, and Qwerty — went to sleep in the lower bunk until it was time to wake up for school.

In the morning we had to rush, my least favorite activity. Mom and Dad blamed the destruction of the garbage and the pillow on Qwerty, who, I have to admit, did look awfully guilty.

Dad said some dogs get crazy scared during thunderstorms.

Elizabeth said she gets a little scared during them, too.

"Not me," I said.

Mom and Dad smiled proudly at me. Dad said they'd see about some repair work during the day on Wingnut, which made Elizabeth do a victory dance about the fact that I had found Wingnut again.

And then I had my last day as a third grader.

Four kids tied for June Superstars. I was one of them. I got a squishy face shrunken head as a prize, which was worth the wait. Ms. Termini came around and gave every student a private compliment during our class party. The compliment I got was "I learned more from you than you learned from me this year, Justin." I tried to assure her I learned stuff, too, like 3×8 and don't hang by my knees, but she was already on to Gianni Schicci. I have no idea what compliment he could have gotten.

Because what I was doing was noticing that it was three fifteen. So third grade was officially finished.

—

June 19, Saturday

My party was good.

Even though Mom didn't let us put eggs inside the rooster piñata. Dad pointed out that roosters actually can't even lay eggs, but Elizabeth agreed with me that it would be so great to have eggs come falling out of the bottom of the rooster when it got smashed.

Mom even said no to a compromise of hard-boiled eggs.

Other than that, the party was good.

So now I guess I am a fourth grader, or at least a fourth-grader-to-be. As we were brushing our teeth tonight, Elizabeth asked if I'd figured out what my third-grade goal was. I said yes, but I was keeping it to myself.

"Did you achieve it?"

"I think so," I said.

"Was it finding Wingnut?" she asked.

"Sort of," I told her. "I think I found Wingnut partly because I had achieved my goal, maybe."

Then she bragged a little about her scissors skills and went to bed.

I climbed up to my top bunk and thought:

I got a little braver this year.

I smiled about that accomplishment for a few seconds.

On the other hand, I reminded myself, there are only 87 days until fourth grade starts. Who will my teacher be? Will she like me? What if the work is way harder in fourth grade? Maybe I should study some stuff just in case I forget everything over the summer. Maybe I should try to figure out what to worry about in advance so I won't get new worries sprung on me by surprise.

But then I looked over at Wingnut, sleeping peacefully and a little battered but clean, now, on the Pillow of Honor, and I just decided not to worry yet.

Maybe things will turn out okay, like they did this year. And when they don't, maybe I'll be able to handle it. Like this year.

Maybe not.

Maybe I actually should get a jump on worrying.

But first, for a few days, I am just going to relax.

Go Fish!

The Evolution of
JUSTIN CASE

Take a look at Matthew Cordell's sketches to
see how each of his characters came to life.

NOAH

DAISY

DAD   MOM

GOFISH

RACHEL VAIL

Where did you get the idea for Justin Krzeszewski and his third-grade experience? Do you have anything in common with Justin?

Gary Spector

I started writing *Justin* with one sentence I couldn't stop thinking: *Justin Case is a third-grade boy with worries.*

I loved Justin as soon as I got to know him. He was struggling so mightily to be brave, to cope with the runny-aroundy boys and the girl he sometimes accidentally likes when he forgets to not like her and his too-adorable little sister and the teacher and dog who turn his insides to quaking jelly. He needed me to tell his true story; he was whispering it to me, confiding it—and when a kid like Justin trusts you to tell his story, you have to tell it true. That was my driving force.

Justin is a meticulous kid. His story came out day by day. Some days he had a lot to say, others just a word or two. Sometimes it had me laughing out loud as I typed, and sometimes it broke my heart. By the end, he had become my hero, this little imaginary guy. This kid who thought his worries made him weak had discovered how strong he really was.

Maybe I learned something about bravery through him.

There are so many characters in this story. Did you base any of Justin's classmates on kids you know, or maybe borrow their names?

I try not to use names of real kids—but I do like to borrow little things like the way a kid sits or the things he thinks are cool or the weird worries she might share with me. I treasure the stories I overhear—or other little details I learn from real kids I knew or get to know now.

Justin is absolutely terrified of dogs in this story. Is that a personal fear of yours? And if so, have you gotten over it?

I'm not afraid of dogs—in fact I love them! But my younger son used to be terrified, and watching him conquer that fear was so impressive to me. He is a really brave guy, just like Justin!

Justin's story is so charming and funny. Will we be able to follow him into the fourth grade?

That's top-secret. . . .

What was it like having your story illustrated? Did you work directly with Matthew Cordell?

I've actually never met Matt in person. He had illustrated my picture book *Righty and Lefty: A Tale of Two Feet* and I loved his work. I was so excited he wanted to illustrate *Justin*. I loved seeing his sketches as they evolved. I think his ability to capture complex emotions—like fear mixed with hope and relief (see Justin climbing the rope)—with just some lines of ink is nothing short of brilliant.

Jiggly food is just not natural, but there's always room for Jell-O. Do you eat Jell-O?

No way. Like Justin, I have a fear of food that jiggles.

What age IS too old for stuffties?
There is no such age.

Where did you get the idea for all those weird and awesome playground games?
My incredibly imaginative sons are amazing sources for cool games. I think in general kids make up games that are more complex and interesting—and way more fun—than the games we grown-ups make them play. That's why I borrow from my guys (with permission only!), and also why I make sure they have plenty of time to invent their own stuff.

What did you want to be when you grew up?
A spy. Or, before that, a teenager.

When did you realize you wanted to be a writer?
While I was writing my second novel.

What's your first childhood memory?
I remember negotiating with my mom about not wanting to give up my bottle.

What was your worst subject in school?
Band. Maybe because I never practiced the saxophone and lived in terror of having to play, which happened every single Wednesday and Friday.

What was your best subject in school?
English and social studies.

What was your first job?
I performed as a clown, running kids' birthday parties.

How did you celebrate publishing your first book?
I did a lot of jumping around and hugging people. And then I took copies to teachers who had made me into a writer.

Where do you write your books?
Sometimes I sit on my couch; sometimes I go to cafes with my laptop. Sometimes I am writing in my mind while I bake banana bread or go for a run or take a shower.

Where do you find inspiration for your writing?
Everywhere I look, and some places I don't.

Which of your characters is most like you?
They are all like me—especially the characters I think are most different from me at the start.

When you finish a book, who reads it first?
Usually my sons—they are fantastic editors.

Are you a morning person or a night owl?
I am most efficient in the morning and the most fun at night.

What's your idea of the best meal ever?
Berries straight off the bushes; fresh mozzarella cheese; a fresh baked baguette with olive oil, ripe August tomatoes, some basil and cilantro and sea salt; and dark chocolate and more berries for dessert. And, most important—good friends sharing lots of laughs the whole time.

Which do you like better: cats or dogs?
I am allergic to cats—so definitely dogs!

What do you value most in your friends?
Kindness, intelligence, and humor.

Where do you go for peace and quiet?
Hikes in the woods.

What makes you laugh out loud?
Absurdity.

What's your favorite song?
Three Little Birds by Bob Marley.

Who is your favorite fictional character?
Justin.

What are you most afraid of?
Letting people down.

What time of year do you like best?
This time, always.

What's your favorite TV show?
Friday Night Lights.

If you were stranded on a desert island, who would you want for company?
Depends how long I was planning to be stranded . . .

If you could travel in time, where would you go?
Everywhen.

What's the best advice you have ever received about writing?
Write lousy first drafts. Just put stuff down, all of it, throw everything in there and don't hold back—be completely free and loose. Then revise, revise, revise—be ruthless. Fall in love with your characters and your story—but not your words. Cut

and rewrite and revise and rework it; keep making stuff up until it's true.

What do you want readers to remember about your books?
Things that made them laugh—or think.

What would you do if you ever stopped writing?
I would read a book a day.

What do you like best about yourself?
I'm pretty good at feeling grateful.

What is your worst habit?
Procrastination.

What do you consider to be your greatest accomplishment?
Blurgh. That's a toughie. Maybe I haven't had it yet.

Where in the world do you feel most at home?
Anywhere I find myself with either somebody interesting and kind—or with a good book and a cozy spot to read it.

What do you wish you could do better?
I wish I could write faster. I also wish I could play either guitar or piano.

What would your readers be most surprised to learn about you?
I am terrible at spelling.

GOFISH

MATTHEW CORDELL

What did you want to be when you grew up?
At one point, I honestly wanted to be . . . a ninja. My older brother and I were big into ninjas in the '80s. In my head, I would move to Japan (just Japan, in general) and learn to be a ninja and then that would be my job. A boy can dream, right?

Julie Halpern

When did you realize you wanted to be an illustrator and writer?
I owe it all to my lovely wife, author Julie Halpern. (Who divides her time between writing, mommy-ing, and school librarian-ing). She introduced me to the wonderful world of children's books (as an adult). I've been an artist all my life, but it wasn't until, oh, the year 2000 or so, because of Julie, that I thought, "This is something I would really like to do."

What's your first childhood memory?
I was one of those kids that always had a pacifier in his mouth. Actually, I always had one there, and I carried one in each hand. I got busted playing some sort of game in the bathroom dipping my "passy" in the toilet and popping it

back in my mouth. Not sure why I was doing that. Sadly, that part of the memory is lost.

What's your most embarrassing childhood memory?
In all fairness, this is not that bad, but it was probably when I was just about to win our school spelling bee in the second grade. I was standing up onstage in front of the whole school, terrified, when I totally choked on "anchor" (I left off the H). In retrospect, it was for the better. I don't know how I would've handled taking my gift for spelling any further.

What's your favorite childhood memory?
I was very close to my grandmother, or Nana, as we called her. My brother and I had many sleepovers at her little apartment, and she was just such a kind, warm soul. So much love and laughter. And as rowdy as we got, she never once laid down any punishment.

As a young person, who did you look up to most?
My mom and dad were both loving and encouraging in their own ways, so to play fair, I would say it was Mom *and* Dad.

What was your worst subject in school?
Once that competitive spirit in kids kicked in, I pretty much lost interest in gym class.

What was your best subject in school?
Definitely art.

What was your first job?
I had this all-purpose job at a little dive restaurant within a golf course. I was a fry cook, a cashier, a custodian, and a dishwasher. It's where I learned how to drive—a golf cart. And not well.

How did you celebrate publishing your first book?

My first picture book, *Toby and the Snowflakes*, was written by Julie, so we got to celebrate as husband and wife. It was very special. By coincidence, on the same day we got news our book was to be published, we were leaving for a trip to Italy. So we had a nice week in Rome and Florence with that good news in our brains.

Where do you write your books?

I divide my work time as both an author and an illustrator between my home office and our local library. I get pretty weird if I work at home, alone, too much. So when I can, I take my laptop and art supplies to the library to be around some people. Good for the soul.

Where do you find inspiration for your writing?

I used to mine the old childhood memories. Which is not always easy. Remembering things and remembering how it felt to be a kid can, for me, get a little muddled. But now, I get lots of inspiration from our two-year-old, Romy. She's an absolute wealth of kidspiration.

Which of your characters is most like you?

In my book *Trouble Gum,* there are two pigs that are brothers. Both have a little of me in them. Ruben is a bit of an innocent troublemaker. And little brother Julius is a silent, but when need be, devious partner-in-crime. I'm a bit of both of those guys.

When you finish a book, who reads it first?

With my writing, I'm a little more sensitive about sharing. I read it about a thousand times myself, editing it over and over, and then I tentatively share it with Julie. Then I tentatively share with my editor. With my art, I'm a bit more confident in the making of. Not quite as much self-editing involved, and less tentative sharing with Julie and then editor.

Are you a morning person or a night owl?
As many times as I've hoped for or tried, I am no morning person. And the older I get, it's harder to keep the night owl thing going too. I guess this leaves me an aspiring morning person.

What's your idea of the best meal ever?
I'm not super picky about food. And I don't eat much meat. I was a vegetarian for over fifteen years, but recently gave in to eating the occasional chicken or turkey. I like spicy food. So . . . spicy, mostly vegetarian food is best. Indian food is pretty yum for this.

Which do you like better: cats or dogs?
I grew up with and have loved both. But, at this point in my life, I prefer the cat for his low maintenance, not-too-clingy personality.

What do you value most in your friends?
Humility and humor.

Where do you go for peace and quiet?
Home, sweet, home.

What makes you laugh out loud?
I'm not a huge belting, laugh-out-loud type of guy. I love to laugh, but I guess I'm picky. Good, funny writing makes me laugh. Julie's books always get me going. Nick Hornby makes me laugh. Also TV like *Parks and Recreation* and *Curb Your Enthusiasm*, and *Freaks and Geeks.* That vibe of humor gets me.

What's your favorite song?
Oh, this changes so often for me. At the time of writing this, it's "Pancho and Lefty" by Townes Van Zandt.

Who is your favorite fictional character?
Overall, and perhaps more out of nostalgia, I'm pretty fond of Spider-Man. Good story. Brainy kid comes to power, and by personal tragedy realizes he must use this power for some good purpose. I love the iconic look of the character too. Nowadays, I don't follow the comics, but as a kid I sure did. And the guy has a way of sticking with you.

What are you most afraid of?
I am pretty terrified of being in high-up places. Looking down is not good.

What time of year do you like best?
I love the springtime. It's the end of winter, which is always good, and it's the start of something new and warm and bright. Just the best feeling of hopefulness in those spring-time months.

What's your favorite TV show?
This changes pretty often for me as well. At the moment, I'm in love with *Parks and Recreation*. So funny and clever. Razor-sharp writing. A superb ensemble.

If you were stranded on a desert island, who would you want for company?
My wife and kid, please. I could not do without the loves of my life.

If you could travel in time, where would you go?
Probably ancient Egypt. Some really weird, really creepy stuff going on there. Sure would be cool to see what that was all about.

What's the best advice you have ever received about writing or illustrating?
In general, as an author/illustrator of picture books, one of the best things I've learned is the whole "show don't tell" philosophy when combining words and pictures for kids. You don't need fifty words to describe something when you have good visual aids. I actually still need to be reminded of this from time to time.

What do you want readers to remember about your books?
Pretty much everything I do is infused with humor. I hope they laugh in the appropriate places and remember my books for being funny.

What would you do if you ever stopped illustrating and writing?
I don't ever want to stop doing this. I'd be heartbroken.

What do you like best about yourself?
I like to think I'm a pretty patient person. I try to be positive and understanding of others. It doesn't always work, as such, but I try.

What is your worst habit?
I have a nervous habit of biting at the ends of my fingers— the cuticles. It's really disgusting, now that I think about it. When I'm watching a stressful movie or something on television. It drives my wife crazy.

What do you consider to be your greatest accomplishment?
My family. Wife and daughter. It takes a lot to balance and make things work and keep people happy and satisfied. And it doesn't always work. But then it does. My life is great because of our little unit.

Where in the world do you feel most at home?
I grew up in a small town in South Carolina. For a long time, it was home. In my mid-twenties, I moved to Chicago, but Carolina still seemed like home. In my early thirties, I moved to the burbs of Chicago. Now this is it. I'm home.

What do you wish you could do better?
I am my worst critic, when it comes to my artwork. When I finish a book, I always wish I had done something better or different. It can be pretty unhealthy, but it does keep me in check I suppose. Well, maybe I wish I were better at not over-criticizing myself.

What would your readers be most surprised to learn about you?
I've never taken a single pen and ink or watercolor class. Completely self-taught in my artistic medium of choice!

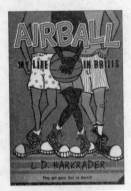